P9-DYY-285

A DARK ROOM.
A STRANGE FEAR.
A TERRIBLE TRAGEDY.

Nick was still in the bedroom, heading for the hall, when he suddenly paused in midstride.

That ominous silence he had noticed downstairs struck him again, only stronger this time. His head felt strangely full. He wondered for a moment if he hadn't accidentally drunk something alcoholic after all, even though he knew his uneasiness had nothing to do with booze.

A seed of fear began to form deep in his mind. The feeling of *heaviness*, inside and out, was not entirely new to him. He had experienced it once before, two years earlier. But that had been in the middle of the night in a dark alleyway after a gang fight that had bought his best friend a switchblade through the heart.

He had not thought of Tommy since he had moved to this new neighborhood. Why now? He did not know. He did not care. He just wanted to get out of the room, back to the others.

Nick strode into and down the hallway. He didn't pause at any of the doors along the way.

He had reached the top of the stairs when the shot exploded in his ears.

No. Lord, please, no.

Books by Christopher Pike

FALL INTO DARKNESS
FINAL FRIENDS #1: THE PARTY
FINAL FRIENDS #2: THE DANCE
FINAL FRIENDS #3: THE GRADUATION
GIMME A KISS
LAST ACT
REMEMBER ME
SCAVENGER HUNT
SEE YOU LATER
SPELLBOUND

Available from ARCHWAY Paperbacks

Most Archway Paperbacks are available at special quantity discounts for bulk purchases for sales promotions, premiums or fund raising. Special books or book excerpts can also be created to fit specific needs.

For details write the office of the Vice President of Special Markets, Pocket Books, 1230 Avenue of the Americas, New York, New York 10020.

Christopher Pike's
FINAL FRIENDS

Book 1: The Party

AN ARCHWAY PAPERBACK
Published by POCKET BOOKS
New York   London   Toronto   Sydney   Tokyo   Singapore

This book is a work of fiction. Names, characters, places and incidents are either the product of the author's imagination or are used fictitiously. Any resemblance to actual events or locales or persons, living or dead, is entirely coincidental.

AN ARCHWAY PAPERBACK *Original*

An Archway Paperback published by
POCKET BOOKS, a division of Simon & Schuster
1230 Avenue of the Americas, New York, NY 10020

Copyright © 1988 by Christopher Pike
Cover art copyright © 1988 Brian Kotzky

All rights reserved, including the right to reproduce
this book or portions thereof in any form whatsoever.
For information address Pocket Books, 1230 Avenue
of the Americas, New York, NY 10020

ISBN: 0-671-73678-7

First Archway Paperback printing September 1988

13 12 11 10 9 8 7 6

AN ARCHWAY PAPERBACK and colophon are
registered trademarks of Simon & Schuster.

Printed in the U.S.A.

IL 9+

For Ashley

The Party

CHAPTER ONE

I should never have gone on vacation in Europe, Jessica Hart thought. *After climbing the Matterhorn, starting high school again feels ridiculous.*

The day was a Friday, the last day of the first week of school, but Jessica's first glimpse of Tabb High. Less than twenty hours earlier she had been enjoying the crisp, cool air of Switzerland's Alps. Now she had Southern California's worst to breathe; the morning was as smoggy as it was hot. Plus she had a terrible case of jet lag. She probably should have skipped what was left of the school week and rested up over Saturday and Sunday, but she had been anxious to see her friends and to check out the place where she was doomed to spend her one and only senior year. So far it had not impressed her.

"I want to have a party," Alice McCoy was saying to her as they wove through the crowds in the outdoor hallway toward Jessica's locker room. "We could get, say, thirty kids from Mesa, with thirty kids from Tabb."

Mesa High had been their alma mater until midsummer, when those in power had decided that the district could not afford two partially full high schools. Tabb had absorbed perhaps three-quarters of Mesa's students. Although Tabb was older than Mesa, it was far bigger. The other twenty-five percent had ended up at Sanders High, five miles farther inland. Fortunately for Jessica, the majority of her friends had moved with her to Tabb, not the least of whom was Alice McCoy. Two years younger, she was—in Jessica's unbiased opinion—the sweetest girl in the whole world.

"You mean as a get-to-know-each-other sort of thing?" Jessica asked.

"Yeah. I think it would help break the ice between us."

"I wouldn't worry about any ice today," Jessica said, brushing her dark hair off her sweaty forehead. On hot days like this she wished she had Alice's bright blond curls; they seemed to reflect most of the sun's rays. "Does this joint have air-conditioning?" Jessica asked.

"In some of the rooms."

"Some?"

"The teachers' lounge is real cool. I was in there yesterday. They want me to paint a mural on the wall." Alice laughed. "They want a mountain glacier."

"It figures. I hope you're charging them?"

"I'm not."

"Fool. Back to this party business. How would you know which thirty Tabb kids to invite?"

Alice nodded. "That's a problem. But maybe in the next week we'll meet some neat people. Have you run into anyone that you like yet?"

Jessica shook her head. "No, and I've been here all of thirty minutes. But maybe by lunch I'll get some guy to fall in love with me."

The words came out easily, but were accompanied by a slight feeling of uneasiness. She had gone on few dates while at Mesa High. Guys just didn't ask her out much. Her best friend, Sara Cantrell, said it was because they were intimidated by her beauty.

"You're right, Sara, that must be it. All those guys watching me from across campus and thinking to themselves that there's a babe beyond their reach. Really, they have a lot of nerve even looking at me."

Actually, Jessica knew she was pretty. Enough people had told her so for enough years, and they couldn't all be wrong. Besides, she had only to look in the mirror. Her face was a perfect oval, with a firm chin and a wide, full mouth that she had trained to smile even when she didn't feel much like smiling. Her hair and eyes matched beautifully. The former was dark brown, long and wavy, with a sheen that had stayed with her from infancy; the latter, an even darker brown, large and round, giving her either a playful or nasty look, depending on her mood. And with a carefully controlled diet and daily jogs around the park, she kept her figure slim and supple. She'd even picked up a tan this summer.

I sound practically perfect!

But, no, she wasn't perfect. She believed, like most teenage girls who don't date much, that there was something wrong with her, something missing. Yet she didn't know what it could be. She didn't understand how Alice—a nice enough looking girl, but certainly no fairy princess—drew girls and guys alike to her in droves. Some people were charismatic, she supposed, and others weren't, and that was that.

Just then Jessica caught sight of a girl in a cheerleader's uniform standing beside a tree and chatting with a group of what appeared to be football players. A stab of envy touched her. The past spring she had success-

3

fully tried out for the cheerleading squad. And all summer she had been looking forward to entering the mainstream of her school's social life. But then *her* school had disappeared, and those who decided such things—who were those jerks, anyway?—had felt that Tabb High should be allowed to maintain its pep squads without integrating those from Mesa High.

God, now there's a girl that looks out of reach.

Jessica stopped Alice, gestured in the direction of the cheerleader. Her blond hair teased and high-lighted, the girl appeared hip, arrogant in a flirty way. Even from a distance, Jessica could see the eyes of the guys gathered around her flickering down her long tanned legs. "Who is that?" she said.

"Clair Hilrey," Alice replied. "Funny you should ask. She was one person I had already decided should come to my party."

"Why?"

"She knows everybody. She's probably the most popular girl on campus. She's gorgeous, isn't she?"

Jessica had already taken a dislike to her. It had been a dream of Jessica's, since her freshman year, that she might be nominated homecoming queen. Back at Mesa, she would have had an excellent chance. Here it already looked as if the odds were stacked against her. She shrugged, started up the hallway again. "She's all right."

Jessica had been at her locker half an hour earlier to deposit her notebook before checking in with her senior counselor. The man had seemed nice enough, but sort of slow and boring, and she couldn't remember his name any more than she could now remember her locker combination. Stopping in front of the locker, she searched her pockets for the slip of paper with the three magic numbers.

"Whoever you put on your list," she said, finding

the paper and twisting the steel dial, "be sure to invite that new guy you're seeing. What's his name, Kent?"

Alice looked doubtful. "Clark. I don't know if he'd come. He doesn't like to be around a lot of people."

The dial felt as if it had gum stuck under it. This school was gross. "Where does he take you when you two go out, the desert?"

Alice smiled briefly. "We don't really go out. He just comes over." She added quickly, almost nervously, "He's an incredible artist. He's helped me so much with my painting."

Jessica paused, studied her. The topic of Clark disturbed Alice, and Jessica wondered why. More than that, she was concerned. She had always felt the urge to take care of Alice. Perhaps because Alice had lost both her parents when she was only ten.

"I'll have to meet him someday," she said finally, brushing a curl of hair from Alice's face. The younger girl nodded, kissed Jessica quickly on the cheek, and began to back away.

"I'm glad you had a happy vacation. I'm even more glad you're home! Catch you later, OK?"

"At lunch. Where should we meet?"

Alice had already begun to slip into the crowd. "I'll find you!" she called.

After waving a quick farewell, Jessica turned and opened her locker and discovered that the light blue cashmere sweater her mother had bought for her in Switzerland for two hundred francs was being spotted with *somebody's* grape juice. The juice was leaking from a soggy brown-paper lunch bag perched on top of a thick notebook that didn't belong to her and which she felt by all rights did not belong in her locker.

"Damn" she whispered, hastily pulling the bag and the notebook out of the locker and dumping them on the ground. Her face fell as she unfolded her prize gift and held it up. She had known it was to be in the high nineties today; she'd only brought the sweater to show off to her friends. Now it had a big stain over the heart area. It was dark enough to be a bloodstain. Suddenly she wished she had never gotten on that plane in Zurich.

"Excuse me, I think these are mine," somebody said from below her. There was a guy crouched down at her feet, picking up the notebook and lunch bag. When he had his things in hand, he glanced up, clearing his throat. "Are we sharing the same locker?"

Jessica let her sweater down and sighed. "You mean you don't even get your own locker in this school? What kind of place is this? I had my own locker in kindergarten."

The guy stood, frowning as he noticed the juice dripping from his bag. "I guess it does take some getting used to. But I don't think I'll be getting in your way much. I only keep my books in my locker."

"And your lunch."

The fellow noticed her sweater and did a quick double take, from it to his bag. "Oh, no, did my grape juice leak on your sweater?"

"Somebody's grape juice did."

He grimaced. "I'm sorry, I really am. Do you think the stain will come out?"

"I'll probably have to cut it out."

"That's terrible." He reached a hand into the bag. "It's all my fault. Boy, can I make it up to you? Could I buy you a new one?"

"Not around here."

"Well, how much did it cost? I could pay you for it at least."

"Two hundred Swiss francs."

"How much is that?"

"I don't know." Jessica leaned an elbow on the wall

6

of lockers, rested her head in her hand, blood pounding behind her temples. What a lousy way to start the day, the whole school year for that matter. "I can't remember."

The guy stood staring at her for a moment. "I really am sorry," he repeated.

Jessica closed her eyes briefly, taking a deep breath, getting ahold of herself. She was making a mountain out of a molehill. Fatigue often made her overreact. Chances were the dry cleaners could get the stain out. And if they didn't, they didn't. Her bedroom closet was overflowing with clothes. When she thought about it, she realized she had little right to blame this guy. After all, she was invading his territory. He had probably had this locker since he was a freshman.

She straightened up, letting the sweater dangle by her side, out of the way. "Don't worry about it," she said. "I have another one at home just like it." She offered him her hand, lightening her tone. "My name's Jessica Hart. I'm a Mesa High refugee."

The guy shook her hand. "I'm Michael Olson."

"Pleased to meet you, Michael." She wondered if this were their first meeting. She could have sworn she had seen him before. "Are you a senior?"

"Yeah."

"So am I."

"I thought so. Did you just get here? I didn't see you earlier this week."

"Yeah, my family's vacation ran a few days too long."

Michael nodded, looking her straight in the face, and as he did, Jessica realized that, besides seeming familiar, he was rather attractive. He had thick black hair and eyebrows, pleasant friendly features. Yet it was his eyes that sparked her interest. There was an extraordinary alertness and intelligence in them, a

7

sharpness she had never seen before in anyone her age. But perhaps she was imagining it. For all she knew, he could be the local druggie, high on something.

But he seems nice enough.

"I bet you were in Switzerland," he said.

She laughed. "How did you guess?"

"Your accent." He glanced about. "I suppose this place looks old to you after Mesa."

She nodded. "And crowded. And hot. We had air-conditioning."

"Some of our rooms are cooled. The gym is. We take our basketball very seriously here at Tabb."

Jessica brightened. "Oh, now I know who you are! You're on the basketball team. I saw you playing last year. You killed us, didn't you?"

Michael shrugged. "It was close most of the way."

"Yeah, right, all through warm-up."

"Well, you guys were never very nice to our football team. What did we lose to you, the last nine in a row?"

"The last ten. And you know what's worse? Practically our whole varsity was transferred to Sanders High."

"I guess we couldn't expect to get beauty and brawn both."

Did he just compliment me? It sounded like a compliment.

Jessica didn't take compliments well. To simply accept them, she felt, was to acknowledge that her looks were important to her, and she always thought that was the same as saying to the world that she was superficial. On the other hand, she did love to be complimented. She was nuts, she knew it.

She laughed again. "Before the football season's

over, I know you're going to think Tabb got the raw end of the deal."

"I hope not," he muttered, lowering his head, pulling a handkerchief from his pocket, and wiping up the few remaining drops of juice from the locker. "I'm going to pay you for that sweater no matter what you say. What's a Swiss franc in U.S. money these days?"

"One and a half pennies. Forget about it, really. I have parents who can't spend enough on their darling daughter."

"It must be nice. Did you enjoy Switzerland?"

"Yeah. And the Greek islands. It was neat floating on a raft in the Mediterranean. The Vatican was far-out, too."

He nodded, repeated himself. "It must be nice." Then he began to back up. "Well, I have to go. I hope you like Tabb. I'm sure you will. If you need help finding your way around, just let me know."

"Thanks, Michael. See you later."

"Sure."

Michael was gone no more than ten seconds when Sara Cantrell appeared. It had been Sara who had been kind enough to pick Jessica and her parents up at the airport at three that morning. Sara had grumbled about it, naturally, but that was to be expected, and wasn't to be taken seriously. The two of them went back to the beginnings of time; they had taught each other to talk. Or rather, Jessica had learned to talk, and Sara had learned to make astute observations. Sara had a biting wit and was usually hungry for potential victims. Tabb High did not yet know what it had inherited. It would know soon, though.

"Hello, Jessie, can't believe you dragged yourself in today. God, you look wasted. You should go home and put your face back under a pillow."

Jessica yawned. "I didn't even go to bed. I was too

busy unpacking. What are you doing here? When you dropped us off at home, you said you were taking the day off.''

"I was until I remembered my mom wasn't working today. She would just drive me nuts. Hey, do you know who that guy you were talking to is?"

"Michael Olson."

"Yeah. I hear he's the smartest guy in the school. Better get on good terms with him. You're taking chemistry, and I hear our young Olson wrote the lab manual they use here.''

"Are you serious? I thought he looked clever." Then she winced. "Did you really sign me up for chemistry?''

"You told me to."

"My *dad* told you to. What do I need chemistry for?"

"So you can get into Stanford and find a smart young man to marry who'll give you smart little kids to play with in a big stupid house.''

Jessica groaned. "I didn't know that's why I was taking chemistry.''

Sara pointed to her sweater. "Did your ears explode while going up in the plane or what? That looks like a bloodstain.''

"I didn't get it on the trip. It's something old. I got it at Penney's.''

Sara grabbed the tag. "Is Penney's charging us in francs these days?''

Jessica pulled the sweater away and shut it in the locker. "Don't hassle me, all right? I'm still getting acclimated." She wiped at the grape juice on her hands. "Last night you said we share first period. What class is it? I lost my schedule already.''

Sara wrinkled her nose. She could do a lot with her nose. She had the same control over it that most people had over their mouths. This did not mean, however, that it was an unusually large nose. Sara was cute. By her own estimation—and Sara could be as ruthless on herself as she was on everybody else—she rated an eight on a scale of one to fourteen. In other words, she was slightly above average. She had rust-colored hair, cut straight above her shoulders, hazel eyes, and a slightly orange tan that somehow got deeper in the winter. Because she frequently wore orange tops and pants to complement her coloring, Jessica told her she looked like Halloween.

"Political science," Sara said. "And we've got this real liberal ex-vet for a teacher. He was in Vietnam and slaughtered little babies, and now he wants us selling the communists hydrogen bombs so he can have a clear conscience."

"He sounds interesting." Jessica didn't believe a word of it. "Come on, let's get there before the bell rings. I'm already four days late."

The teacher's name was Mr. Bark, and Sara hadn't been totally off base in her analysis. The first thing the man did when they were all seated was dim the lights and put on a videotape of a nuclear attack. The footage was from the big TV movie *The Day After*. They watched a solid ten minutes of bombs exploding, forests burning, and people vaporizing. When the lights were turned back on, Jessica discovered she had a headache. World War III always depressed her. Plus she wasn't wearing her glasses as she was supposed to; watching the show had strained her eyes. Sitting to her right, Sara had put her head down and nodded off. Jessica poked her lightly, without effect. Sara continued to snore softly.

"I hope my purpose in showing this tape is clear," Mr. Bark began, leaning his butt on the edge of his desk. "We can *talk* on and on about how incredibly destructive nuclear weapons are, but I think what we have just seen creates an image of horror that will stay with us a long time, and will remind us that above all else we can't allow the political tensions of the world to reach the point where pushing the button becomes a viable alternative."

If Sara hadn't been lying about his being a vet, then Mr. Bark hid it well. He didn't look like someone who had seen battle. In fact, he looked remarkably like a plump, balding middle-aged man who had taught high school political science all his life. He had frumpy gray slacks, black-rimmed glasses, and an itch on his inner left thigh that he obviously couldn't wait to scratch.

Jessica poked her friend again. Sara turned her head in the other direction and made a low snorting sound.

"One Trident submarine," Mr. Bark continued, raising one finger in the air for emphasis, striding down the center of the class, "has the capacity to destroy two hundred Soviet cities. Think about it. And think what would happen if the captain of a Trident sub should go off half-cocked and decide to make a place in history for himself, or to put an end to all history. Now I know most of you believe that the fail-safe device the president has near him at all times controls—"

We should have had someone else pick us up at the airport.

Mr. Bark paused in midstride, suddenly realizing he didn't have Sara's full attention. Impatience creased his wide fleshy forehead. He moved to where he stood above her.

"She had a late night," Jessica said.

Mr. Bark frowned. "You're the new girl? Jessica Hart?"

"Yes, sir."

"And you're a friend of Sara's?"

"Yes, sir."

"Would you wake her, please?"

"I'll try." Jessica leaned close to Sara's head, hearing scattered giggles from the rest of the class. Putting her hand on the back of Sara's neck, she whispered in her ear, "You are making fools of both of us. If you don't wake up this second, I am going to pinch you."

Sara wasn't listening. Jessica pinched her. Sara sat up with a bolt. "Holy Moses," she gasped. Then she saw the stares, the smirks. Unfazed, she calmly leaned back in her chair and picked up her pen as if to take notes, saying, "Could you please repeat the question, Mr. Bark?"

"I didn't ask a question, Sara."

Sara stifled a yawn. "Good."

"But I'll ask one now. Were you awake through any of the videotape?"

"I got the highlights."

"I'm glad. Tell me, what was your gut reaction while watching the bombs explode?"

Sara smiled slowly. "I thought it was neat."

Mr. Bark shook his head. "You might think you are being funny, but I can assure you that you are—"

"No, no," Sara interrupted. "I'm telling you exactly how I felt. The whole time I was watching it, before I nodded off, I was thinking, Wow."

Mr. Bark grinned in spite of himself. "Granted, Sara, the visual effects were outstanding. But didn't the wholesale destruction of our civilization upset you?"

"No."

"Come on, be serious. I had girls crying when I showed this tape in fifth period yesterday."

"Mr. Bark," Sara replied with a straight face, "when I was watching that part where the bomb exploded outside that university, I honestly thought to myself, 'Why, those lucky kids. They won't have to go to school anymore.' "

The class burst out laughing. Mr. Bark finally gave up. He tried to dig up more heartfelt testimonials from the less bizarre minded, and while he did so, Jessica noticed a handsome blond fellow sitting in the corner. She had to fight not to stare. What kind of place was this Tabb? First there was Clair Hilrey, who belonged in *Playboy,* and now there was this hunk. It was a wonder that they couldn't put together a halfway decent football team with all these great genes floating around. She poked Sara again.

"Who's that in the corner?" she whispered.

"The football quarterback," Sara whispered back.

"What's his name?"

"He hasn't got one. But his jersey number is sixteen."

"Tell me, dammit."

"William Skater, but I call him Bill. Pretty pretty, huh?"

"Amazing. Do you know if he has a girlfriend?"

"I've seen him hanging out with this cheerleader named Clair."

"God, I hate this school."

"Miss Hart?" Mr. Bark called.

"Yes, sir?"

He wanted to know about her feelings on radiation, and of course, she told him she thought it was just awful stuff. When the class was over, Jessica did her best to catch Bill's eye, but he wasn't looking.

I've been here less than two hours. I can't be getting a crush on someone already.

She ditched Sara and trailed Bill halfway across campus. He had a great ass.

*   *   *

The following period was the dread chemistry, and the teacher's lecture on molecular reactions proved far harder to absorb than Mr. Bark's on atomic explosions. This was definitely one class she wouldn't be able to BS her way through.

Toward the middle of the period, they started on the first lab of the year. Jessica ended up with a quiet Hispanic girl named Maria Gonzales for a partner. They hardly had a chance to talk, but she struck Jessica as the serious type. Jessica just hoped she was smart and took excellent notes. She wondered if Michael Olson really was a wizard at science. It would be asking too much, she supposed, to hope William Skater was.

Maybe Bill will be in another one of my classes.

Break came next. Before leaving for school that morning, Jessica had spoken to another friend of hers, Polly McCoy—Alice's older sister—filling her in on everything that had happened on her vacation. She had known Polly almost as long as she had Sara, although she was not nearly so close to Polly. A lot of their friendship was founded on simple geography; since they were kids they had lived only a few hundred yards apart; it was hard not to be friends with someone your own age who lived so close.

Polly had what at best could be described as a nervous disposition. It showed particularly when she was around Sara, who enjoyed picking on Polly. Keeping the two girls apart was difficult, however, because none of them really had any other close friends, and they usually ended up going to movies, the beach, or wherever together. Three bored girls each looking for one exciting guy.

When Polly and Alice's parents had died, they left the girls a large construction company. It was at present managed by a board of directors, but both girls were potential bosses and millionaires. They lived in a big house with a partially senile aunt who was their legal guardian. They lived as they wanted. Only the McCoy sisters could think of throwing a party to introduce two schools to each other.

But it turned out that Alice had not told Polly about the party.

"She's going to do what?" Polly asked as they waited in line at the soda machines. Polly had already gotten ahold of a candy bar. She ate a lot of sweets these days, and it showed, especially in her face. It was a pity. When thin, Polly was a doll.

"She's going to invite thirty of our own people and team them up with thirty of Tabb's people," Jessica said, casting an eye toward the front of the line. Apparently the machines here took kicks as well as quarters. The guy up front was busting a toe for a Coca-Cola Classic.

"She never told me."

"Maybe she just thought it up."

"I don't care. We're not having it. They'd rip up the house."

"No, they wouldn't." The guy kicked the machine one final time and then stalked off. He was from Mesa. "But let's not invite that guy. Hey, is there another place we can get something to drink?"

"There's the mall. It's less than five minutes away in the car. But I don't want to go there now. And I don't want a party at my house."

Jessica decided she'd let Sara and Alice argue with Polly. She had already made up her mind that they had to have the party if only to invite Mr. Football Quarterback. "All right, all right, we'll have it in my bedroom. What did you do while I was gone?"

"Nothing." Polly took a bite of her candy, her

bright green eyes spanning the jammed courtyard. Then she grinned. "I take that back. I did do something funny. They were running a contest on the radio to see who could send in the best album cover for a new heavy-metal band. I can't even remember the group—it was Hell and Steel something. Anyway, I sent in one of Alice's paintings. She won!"

"What did she win?"

"A free trip to one of their New York shows and a backstage pass. The disc jockey said the group is seriously considering using her artwork."

"Is Alice going to go?"

"No. You know she hates loud music."

"Wait a second. One of Alice's paintings on the album cover of a heavy-metal band? Since when does she paint anything that doesn't have flowers and clouds in it?"

Polly shrugged. "It's none of my business."

"What's none of your business?"

"What Clark has her drawing."

"Her boyfriend has her drawing whips and demons? Boy, I hope he hasn't seduced her."

Polly did not appreciate the remark. She was fanatically protective of her younger sister. "He's not her boyfriend. He's just someone who comes over and eats our food."

"What's he look like?"

"Not bad, pretty good."

"You wouldn't want to give me too many details, would you?"

Polly smiled. Unlike her sister, her hair was dark, almost black, with red highlights. Indeed, in almost every respect, their looks differed. Alice was a waif. Polly was a peasant. She had big breasts and a bigger butt. "He's got great hands," she said.

"How do you know?"

"I'm not saying anything."

"For someone who doesn't like to pry into Alice's business, you've said a lot." The subject was beginning to bore Jessica. She noticed a booth near the center of campus, pointed it out. "What can we sign up for over there?"

Now Polly was bored. "Student office. They've lengthened lunch today so all those who want to play politics can tell us why we should vote for them. You're not thinking of running for anything, are you?"

Jessica had a brilliant idea. "No, but Sara is."

"Sara? She doesn't like to get involved in choosing what to wear in the morning."

"You say the candidates are supposed to speak at lunch today?"

"In the gym, yeah. It's the only cool building on campus."

"Let's sign her up."

"We can't. You have to sign up in person."

"Then you be Sara for a few minutes."

"We'll never get her out on the floor to speak."

"We'll worry about that later."

"She'll be furious." Polly paused, thought about that a moment. "All right, I'll be Sara. What should we have her run for?"

"What else? Student body president."

CHAPTER TWO

Michael Olson had not heard Jessica Hart's comment to Alice McCoy about finding a guy to fall in love with by lunch, but had he been listening, he might have believed her to be a beautiful witch capable of casting potent spells. Michael had thought of Jessica, and nothing else, all morning. He had a terrible feeling he was going to spend a substantial portion of the remainder of the year thinking about her.

And I'm going to have to see her every day, several times a day, until June.

Whereas most guys would have been delighted with a setup that would bring them repeatedly in contact with a girl they found attractive, Michael didn't for the simple reason that he knew he'd never be able to get past the hello-how-are-you? stage. It was true that he had said much more to her than that during their first meeting, but that had been before he'd had a chance to fantasize about her. Now just the memory of her made him uneasy. He didn't know what it had been about her that had hit him so hard. He wondered if her effect on him hadn't been largely because of his own

19

state of mind. His summer had been particularly lonely. He had worked and read a lot, and gone out seldom; and never with anyone of the opposite sex. Since school started he'd been looking over the new girls from Mesa. There was no doubt he was ripe for a crush.

Or a heartache.

"Remember that scene in *War Games* when Matthew Broderick changes the girl's grade with his home computer?" Bubba asked as he and Michael strolled across the deserted campus. Fourth period had just begun, but neither Bubba nor Michael was cutting. Because of extremely high scores on IQ tests taken when they were in junior high, both guys were in the MGM (Mentally Gifted Minors) Program. They had a free period each day to pursue individual projects that their superior intelligence qualified them to pursue. In actuality, they probably were cutting. So far this year, they had used fourth period primarily to get an early start on lunch.

"I remember the scene," Michael said. "You couldn't do that here, though, could you?"

Bubba was a wizard at computers, and at life itself. He was five feet four, and because he enjoyed food and denied himself nothing, he was also rather round. But stature and weight were no obstacle to Bubba. He went out with practically any girl he wanted and enjoyed the reputation as the coolest person in Tabb High.

"Not without the codes that give access to the school district's data files."

"I didn't think the scene was very realistic," Michael said. "Hey, why are we going to the administration building?"

"To get the codes."

"What?"

Bubba smiled faintly. He endeavored to maintain a serene countenance, like the holy Buddha, from whom his nickname had been derived. Michael couldn't remember who had thought up the nickname. Perhaps it had been Bubba himself. His real name was John Free.

"Mr. Bark wants me to write a program that will automatically read and count the votes on the cards that will be used in the voting for student body officers," Bubba explained.

"But you don't need the district data files to do that."

"Does Miss Fenway know that?"

Miss Fenway was a secretary in the administration building. "What does Miss Fenway have to do with any of this?"

"She has the codes written on a little piece of white paper taped to a board that slides out from her desk above her top left drawer. I saw them there yesterday."

"Did you memorize them?"

"No, I didn't have a chance. But I will today."

"But what does this have to do with the program you're writing for Mr. Bark?"

"Absolutely nothing."

Once inside the administration building, they went straight to Miss Fenway's office. She was busy sorting files at a corner cabinet when they entered. Michael had always liked Miss Fenway. She enjoyed playing mother to every kid in school, and she took special pride in him because he got straight A's. But she was no dummy, and he doubted Bubba would trick her into giving out confidential information. She had a computer terminal on her desk.

"May I help you boys?" she asked, putting down her papers and stepping toward them. A thin woman

21

with a warm, wrinkled face, she had never married nor had any kids.

"Yes," Bubba said. "Mr. Bark has put me in charge of tabulating the votes for student body officers this afternoon. I need the codes that will allow me to connect the old card reader in this building with the new PC in the computer science class."

Miss Fenway was puzzled. "I hadn't been informed about this."

"Mr. Bark is free this period. You'll find him in the teachers' lounge, I believe. He'll explain what I mean." Bubba took a seat, making it clear he was going to wait in her office until she did what he wanted. Miss Fenway looked at Michael.

"Do you know what this is all about?"

"Not me."

The instant Miss Fenway left, Bubba sprang to his feet—he was remarkably agile given his physique—and closed the door. He had the desk board with the page of codes pulled out in two seconds. Swiftly, but carefully, he began to copy them down.

"I didn't see you do this," Michael said.

"See me do what?"

Miss Fenway returned a minute later with Mr. Bark. The latter explained to Bubba that all he had to do was write a program that broke the count down into freshmen, sophomores, etc. He would do the rest. Bubba nodded and apologized for not understanding the first time. As they were leaving, Mr. Bark told them about a video he wanted them to see.

"From the TV movie *The Day After*?" Bubba asked.

"Yes."

"I've seen it," Bubba said.

"What did you think?"

"It was neat."

Mr. Bark sighed. "I have this new student you should meet."

The computer room was empty fourth period. They had the place to themselves. Using the stolen codes, Bubba called up the files containing the transcripts of every kid in the school district. Michael wondered at his motivation. Although as intelligent as himself, Bubba never worried much about his grades. He had no intention of attending college. He wanted to go straight into business. In fact, he already invested in commodities and stock options. He also bet the horses through his uncle, who was a bookie with mob connections. Financially speaking, Bubba's family occupied the same position as Michael's, lower middle class. And yet Bubba drove an old but well-kept Jaguar and wore only the finest clothes. And he didn't even have a job. Since Michael had to slave six days a week at a local 7-Eleven to help his divorced mother make ends meet, he knew if he were to criticize Bubba's *businesses,* he would only be doing so out of jealousy.

"Here you are," Bubba said, pointing to the screen. Michael leaned closer. Semester after semester—rows of A's, except for one C his junior year. He'd gotten it last year in calculus. A pal of his had desperately whispered for help in the middle of a test. Being such a swell guy, Michael had slipped him a piece of paper with a few answers that, through bad timing and bad luck, had ended up in the hands of the teacher. Regrettably, the test had been the final exam and the teacher had given them both automatic Fs. It had slashed his overall semester grade in half. His hopes of being valedictorian had gone out the window then and there.

"You can't change it," Michael said. "Everyone on the faculty knows I got that C."

Bubba's fingers danced over the keyboard. Then he frowned. "We can't change it, anyway. The file's protected. I should have known. Once transferred to the district offices, the grades are carved in stone." He thought for a moment, then jumped out of the file and into another that was the same except for the absence of recorded grades.

"What's that?" Michael asked.

"This semester's records." Bubba moved the cursor beside Michael Olson's MGM fourth period, put in an A. "This file hasn't been transferred yet. We can manipulate it up until the day it is." He erased the A. "You know, Mike, I think this is going to be a pretty laid-back year for the two of us. Would you like me to pull Dale Jensen's record?"

Dale Jensen had the only grade-point average higher than Michael's. It was a perfect 4.00. But Dale hadn't taken a difficult class in all the time he had gone to Tabb. He specialized in subjects where he could get up and indulge in long-winded monologues about how screwed up all the screw-ups in the world were. He was really a despicable character. If anyone stopped to tell him something, he always interrupted with the sarcastic line "I'm impressed."

"No, leave him alone."

"Are you sure? Who wants to listen to him graduation day?"

"We're not going to sneak a phony grade onto his transcript for this year without him knowing it."

"I suppose you're right," Bubba replied without much conviction, sitting back from the screen and stretching.

"I wanted to tell you about this girl I met," Michael began.

"Ask her out."

"No, let me tell you about her first."

"What for? I'm sure she's the greatest discovery since sliced bread. Just ask her out. What's her name?"

"You probably haven't seen her. She just got here this morning. Jessica Hart."

Bubba nodded approvingly. "I know her, a quality chick. A friend of hers is having a party for the whole school."

"Where did you hear that?"

Bubba shrugged. He seldom revealed the sources of his information. He was seldom wrong about anything. "I don't think you should wait until the party to go after her. She won't last, not around here. Someone will nab her. It may as well be you."

Michael chuckled at the crude manner in which Bubba referred to Jessica. He knew that Bubba had a strong admiration for the female species, or at least a powerful appreciation of them, which was almost the same thing. Girls who went out with Bubba once wanted to go out with Bubba twice. He knew how to satisfy them.

"Why don't you ask her on a date?" Michael asked.

"I can't. I've got to save myself for Clair Hilrey."

"I thought Clair was going with our esteemed quarterback, Bill Skater?"

"They've dated a few times. They went to the Baked Potato Restaurant last Saturday night. But it's nothing serious."

"Does Clair know this?"

"Give me a couple of weeks, and I'll make it clear to her."

Michael scratched his head. "Didn't Clair tell you last spring that she thought you were the most disgusting human being in the whole school?"

"It makes no difference, Over the summer your average teenage girl forgets nine-tenths of what happened the previous school year. I'll ask her out at tonight's game, during halftime. She'll say yes."

Michael shook his head in amazement. "I'm going to enjoy watching this."

Bubba sat up, speaking seriously. "I'll let you in on a profound secret. Only the very elect of males in our society know this. And once you know it and ponder its significance for any length of time, your whole perspective will change."

"The earth is really flat?"

"No." Bubba leaned closer. "Girls want to have sex exactly as much as boys want to."

Michael laughed. "Bubba, I just met Jessie. I don't even know her. I don't want to sleep with her. I'm afraid to talk to her."

"It is much easier to have sex than to talk. When you talk, you have to think. You think too much, Mike. That's your problem. And you're lying to yourself. Of course you want to sleep with Jessie. You don't have to be ashamed. Chances are she probably wouldn't mind sleeping with you if she thought she could do it and not have to pay for it later in some way. That's why girls love me so much. I let them know that with me everything is OK."

"But you kiss and tell. With what you just said, that makes you a hypocrite. Take how you carried on about Cindy Fosmeyer."

"Who do I tell except you? And I know you would never damage a girl's reputation." He smiled. "And since we're talking about Cindy, did I ever tell you she has the hots for you?"

Cindy Fosmeyer had huge breasts. They were so huge they fairly blotted out any personality she might have had. "You never did because it's not true."

"Believe what you want, buddy." Bubba stood.

"But I give you my word on this—if you don't ask Jessica out by Monday, I will."

Michael was not amused. He had known Bubba a long time. They'd had a lot of good times together. But there was a lot about him he didn't know, that he didn't want to know. "Is that a threat?"

"Think of it as an incentive."

"What about saving yourself for Clair?"

Bubba patted his bulging gut. "There's enough of me to go around." He turned toward the door. "I'll be back in a minute."

Bubba was gone much longer than a minute. While waiting, Michael entertained himself scanning Jessica Hart's transcript. He felt mild guilt at prying, but couldn't resist. He was mildly surprised to discover she was taking chemistry. She must have some smarts, but then, he had observed that talking to her. Perhaps she would need a tutor. He knew the subject so well that a rumor had gone around last year that he had written the lab manual. It was incredible the things people would believe.

When the door opened behind him, he assumed it was Bubba. The cool, soft hug from behind caught him by surprise.

"Hi, Mikey!"

"Alice, what are you doing here?"

Michael had met Alice McCoy the previous winter, a couple of weeks before Christmas. Wearing what he was later to discover to be her typical sunny expression, she had popped into his 7-Eleven and asked if she could paint Santa Claus and Frosty the Snowman on his windows. He had been immediately taken by her enthusiasm. She told him he could pay her what he thought it was worth, and if he didn't like it when she was done, he wouldn't have to pay her at all. It sounded like a good deal, but the owners of the store were Muslims from Lebanon, and he didn't know if they'd appreciate Christmas decorations all over their place of business. A quick call dispelled his fears; the two brothers were eager to have their store look as American as possible.

The next day was a Saturday. Alice showed up at nine o'clock in the morning. He expected her to chalk out a few reindeer and spray on a couple of featureless snowmen and call it done. Her supplies threw him for his first loop. She had a huge, flat black case of paints and brushes. She spent a half hour cleaning and polishing the windows before starting, and when she finally did begin, she worked steadily for seven hours, slowly, patiently, meticulously unfolding a rich colorful tapestry of sparkling elves, joyous children, and racing sleighs. When she finished, she sprayed on a sealer that she promised would protect the paintings. When he finally did wash away her work, near Easter, it had been with a heavy heart. But by then he'd had something greater than her pictures to enjoy. He had Alice herself, as both a regular visitor and a good friend. She was a true gift of holiday magic. She had charm and grace, kindness and wit.

She was everything he had imagined his little sister would have been.

Michael's mother was only seventeen and in high school when she had given birth to him. Old man Jerry Olson split for parts unknown five years after that—Michael still had a few clear memories of his dad—and since then his mother had dated a seemingly endless succession of men. Two years ago one of them had gotten her pregnant. The guy had had no wish to marry her—he, too, would eventually disappear—and his mother had vacillated about having an abortion. Finally, over Michael's bitter protests, she had decided on the operation—sort of late. He did not understand why the doctor had told his mom it had been a girl, or why she had told him.

By a strange quirk of fate, he'd always thought of his unborn sister as *Alice*. After the incident, he often dreamed of what she would have been like. His little Alice. He still loved his mother more than anyone, but he doubted he'd ever totally forgive her for what she had done.

But now, with Alice McCoy here to see him, it was easy to pretend what had gone before had been only a bad dream.

"What am I doing? I'm cutting, just like you," she said, releasing him and walking around the room, lightly tapping the keyboards on Tabb's brand-new PCs, touching a printout page. Like a perpetually curious child, Alice was fascinated with everything around her.

"You have an art class now, right?"

"Yeah, I'm supposed to be at the park across the street studying tree branches. But they've just sprayed there with an awful-smelling insecticide." She giggled. "I did start on this one sketch of a giant mosquito sucking the sap out of a tree. It was really gross."

"Can I see it?"

"No."

"Did you throw it away?"

She shook her head. "But I'm going to, right after I show it to Clark. It really is weird. I can't believe I drew it."

"Clark's your new boyfriend, isn't he?"

"He's not that new. I see him a lot."

"I'd like to meet him. What's he like?"

Alice shrugged, tossing her bright head of hair. "I don't want to talk about him. I want to tell you about

29

a friend of mine I want you to meet. She's from Mesa, like me. She's really wonderful.''

"What's her name?"

"I'm not going to tell you. I want to be the one to introduce you so that when you both fall in love, and get married later on, you'll be able to look back and say it was *I* who made it all possible. Are you going to the game tonight?''

"I'm going to try. I have to work, but I should be able to catch the second half.''

"Could you get there at halftime? I could introduce you to her then.''

Michael chuckled. He wasn't really interested in Alice's friend, not after meeting Jessica Hart, but he saw no harm in saying hello to the girl. "What's wrong with today at lunch?''

"I won't be here. I have a doctor's appointment.''

He paused. "What for? I mean, are you sick?''

Alice brushed aside the question. "It's nothing, I just have to stop in.''

"How are you going to get there? I could give you a ride.'' For some reason, the thought of Alice going all alone to the doctor disturbed him. He knew she had no parents, and that her guardian aunt didn't get out often.

"I'm taking a taxi.''

"They're expensive.''

"I have money. Don't worry about it. Just be there tonight at halftime. I'll get her to come.''

"I'll do my best," he promised.

She smiled. "Thanks, this means a lot to me. Oh, what's that you have on your screen? It looks like a report card.''

Michael explained how through the use of special codes—he didn't say where they had obtained them— he and his friend were able to tap into the school's files. Alice was fascinated, but before she could ask any questions, Bubba returned. And when Bubba realized that Alice had been made privy to what he obviously considered inside information, he quickly tried to present a more innocent picture of their doings.

"What's on this screen is only a photocopy of existing records," he said. "It's not the records themselves. We're just looking at them, that's all. It's no big deal."

Alice grinned slyly. "Sure, you're getting ready to turn the school upside down, and it's nothing? I'm not that dumb. Come on, where did you steal these codes?"

"What codes?" Bubba asked, glancing at Michael. "These photocopies aren't confidential. You don't need codes to access them."

Alice laughed gaily, much to Bubba's displeasure. "I don't believe you!"

Bubba feigned nonchalance, quickly maneuvering out of the file, leaving the screen blank. "Suit yourself," he said.

"In fact, I think you could get into lots of trouble if certain people knew about this," Alice said playfully.

Bubba stopped, stared at her a moment. "No one's going to get into trouble. No one's going to talk about this. OK?"

She didn't understand what he was really saying. "He's right," Michael said. "This isn't something that should get around. Do me a favor, Alice, and forget what I showed you here."

"All right," she said cheerfully. "But I know it was all your idea, Bubba. Michael wouldn't fool with people's grades."

"Nor would I," Bubba said curtly.

Alice laughed again, oblivious to the tension in the

31

room. Giving Michael a quick kiss on the cheek, she reminded him to be sure to get to the stadium by halftime. The instant she was gone, Bubba turned off the screen and shook his head.

"Mike, you're not improving your chances of being valedictorian by trying to get us both expelled."

"Alice won't talk. She's my friend."

"Alice is a fifteen-year-old girl who is not my friend. I don't trust her."

"Don't worry about it. She was only kidding."

Bubba thought for a moment. "All right, Mike, whatever you say."

Michael and Bubba went to the mall for lunch shortly after that. It was crowded. Michael remembered when the mall had been nothing but a piddling collection of failing stores. Put a roof over something and people swarmed in.

Michael ordered a turkey sandwich from Ed's Sandwich Selection. His mother was usually too tired after working all day as a secretary in a downtown high-rise to cook; he had grown up eating most of his food wedged between two slices of bread.

He was practically finished with his sandwich before Bubba had even decided what to order. Bubba finally opted for Indian food, which took time to prepare (to his specifications). By then many of Tabb's students had already come and gone so they could be back for the special assembly of candidate speeches. Michael also had a mild interest in hearing the talks. Plus he hoped to run into Jessica Hart again. He had begun to take Bubba's threat seriously. At Michael's prodding, Bubba got his dishes to go.

The assembly was well under way when they entered the gym. The bleachers were jammed. They stood near the ticket booth beside the entrance, Bubba holding his aromatic spiced dahl and rice in a white cardboard container, surveying the audience for a seat. In a high, cracking voice, a girl at the microphone was talking about school spirit and how far-out she was.

"Do you see her?" Bubba asked.

"I'm not looking for her."

"I believe you. I see her."

"Where? Don't point."

"Sixth row on the far right, two rows behind Fosmeyer's body."

Michael saw her. It was amazing how her beauty had magnified since morning. The shine of her long brown hair seemed to jump right out from the crowd. "All right, let's leave," Michael said.

"But you dragged me back here. No, we're going to sit behind her."

Michael didn't like that idea. "There's no room."

Bubba ignored him. "Come on."

They didn't actually get the seats directly behind Jessica, but a couple of rows back. Bubba obtained the space by gesturing to a couple of sophomores to move to the rear. Bubba did not have a reputation for being violent; nevertheless, the kids jumped when he pointed. Climbing the steps, Michael had kept his head turned away from Jessica. He didn't know if she'd noticed him.

Sitting in the row between Michael and Jessica were a couple of Tabb's football players. They cheered loudly as the next speaker was announced: Bill Skater. Bubba began to lay out his Indian delicacies, opening a bottle of Perrier and spreading a cloth napkin across his lap. Michael saw Jessica lean forward as Bill strode toward the microphone. She had a pudgy girl with dark hair on her left and an orange-haired girl on her right. These two girls turned and spoke to Jessica when Bill appeared. Michael leaned forward, trying to block out Bill's opening statements, straining to hear what the girls were saying.

"He walks like a stiff board," the one on the left said.

"I hear he's the worst quarterback in Tabb's long history of terrible quarterbacks," the one on the right said.

"Shut up, both of you," Jessica said.

"Oh, but I think he's cute," the one on the left said.

"He should take his shirt off and give his speech," the one on the right agreed.

"Shh. I want to hear what he has to say," Jessica said.

"What for, we've heard it all before," the one on the left said.

"Yeah, I wish I could get down there and tell them what this school really needs," the one with orange hair said.

This last comment caused Jessica and her pal on the left to break into laughter. Michael didn't know what was so funny. He wondered if Jessica was interested in Bill Skater.

Michael listened to Bill's speech with an open and unprejudiced mind, but never did figure out what he was running for, much less why anyone should vote for him. Bubba continued to savor his meal. When Clair Hilrey's name was announced next, however, Bubba looked up.

"Isn't she something?" he muttered as Clair swaggered to the microphone in her cute blue-and-gold cheerleader uniform.

"She's an empty phony devoid of an iota of intelligence."

Bubba nodded. "True. But if you look past those superficial qualities, you'll see her true value."

34

"Which is?"

"It's hard to express in words. Just imagine her naked."

Clair's speech had a content similar to Bill's, which is to say it had no content at all. But she giggled a lot, whereas Bill had been as stiff as the board Jessica's friend had compared him to, and she did have an alluring way of propping her hands on her hips at the top of her undeniably gorgeous legs. Clair made it clear she wanted to be school president.

The name Sara Cantrell was called next.

"What the hell?" the girl on Jessica's right said.

"Go ahead, tell them what this school really needs," Jessica said.

"No way. I'd have to start by telling them it doesn't need me."

"Coward," the girl to Jessica's left said.

"Don't call me a coward, you spineless fish."

"Sara Cantrell, please?" the announcer repeated.

"It took you three years to alienate everyone at Mesa," Jessica said. "Just think of the power you'll have behind that microphone. You can do it all in one afternoon here."

The logic appealed to the strange girl named Sara. Michael watched as she stood and made her way down the bleacher steps and onto the gymnasium floor.

"Hi, I'm Sara," she began, completely at ease. "I'm not really running for anything. My friends Jessica Hart and Polly McCoy signed me up because they thought it would be funny to get me down here." Sara pointed toward her friends. "They're sitting right over there. Let's give them a big laugh to show them that at least we think *they're* funny."

The audience cheered loudly. Jessica and Polly turned beet red and buried their faces in their knees. Michael burst out laughing.

"But since I am here," Sara continued, "I do have a few things I'd like to say. First, I don't think you should vote for anybody who's spoken this afternoon. They all struck me as a bunch of insecure idiots, looking to get their egos stroked. Second, I don't believe we need student officers at all. What do they do? I'll tell you. Nothing! And finally, I don't know who out there stole the chewing gum from my locker, but I hope you choke on it. Thank you."

Sara received a standing ovation and thunderous applause. She walked back to her place as though she were just another spectator taking her seat. But she grinned when she reached her friends.

"How did I do?" she asked.

"You'll probably be expelled," Polly said.

"Or elected," Jessica said.

"I think your girlfriend's right," Bubba whispered in Michael's ear.

CHAPTER THREE

Nick Grutler did not go to the mall for lunch nor did he attend the afternoon assembly. He didn't own a car to drive anywhere, and no one had told him about the election. Indeed, although Nick had been in school every day since Monday, no one at Tabb had even spoken to him outside of class, and that included his teachers. Nick Grutler was six feet four, wiry as a hungry animal, and as black as midnight. No one had spoken to him for the simple reason that they were afraid of him.

Tabb High had several black students—four to be exact, two girls and two boys—but none of them was a recent transfer from East L.A. where youth gangs ruled. None of them had the pent-up emotion that came from having to master the use of a switchblade by age twelve just to survive. Nick had not killed anybody—no one he had been forced to stab, at least, had died in his presence—but he had seen more violence than most war vets. And he had always hated it, and worse—in his own mind, for someone of his size and strength—had been afraid of it. None of the teachers that had yet to speak to him had noticed that the new boy from the other side of the city who sat so still during class actually had tremors beneath his skin. Nick had a lot he wished he could forget.

But it was his intention to forget, or if that was not possible, at least to put the past behind him. He considered the new job his divorced father had landed in a nearby aerospace firm as a gift from above. Another summer in East L.A. like the past one, Nick knew, probably would have seen him killed. On the other hand, Tabb High was no paradise either, so far.

He was enrolled as a senior, but he had to admit to himself that he hardly qualified as a freshman in this part of town. He was going to have to read the textbooks they had given him. He was going to have to *learn* to read.

He had absolutely no one to talk to. The white kids at school were all caught up in things that he had always imagined were just for TV characters. They went to the beach and parties and worried about what they were going to wear to the next dance. In a way they were like children to him. They had never stared down the barrel of a sawed-off shotgun and been ordered to kiss cold metal. They had lived incredibly sheltered lives. And yet, they were light-years beyond him. They knew all kinds of stuff. They could get up in front of a whole class and speak what was on their minds. They had nice clothes, nice cars, and lots of money. They could laugh at the drop of a hat. He had spent Monday through Thursday feeling superior to them. But now that it was Friday, he realized he was jealous—and all alone.

His counselor had put him in sixth period P.E., where all the athletes were. The only connection Nick had had with any sport was basketball. He used to play in a lot of pick-up games in the inner city. Of course, basketball season was months away. The coach who oversaw the P.E. class hadn't known what to do with him. Finally he'd asked if Nick would like to lift weights. Sure, Nick had said.

Nick was working up a sweat with over two hundred pounds on the bench press that Friday afternoon when the big, fat-legged dude with the thin-lipped mouth began to hassle him.

"A little heavy for you?" the dude asked, taking up a position near Nick's knees. Lying on his back, Nick could see that the weight room was fairly crowded, about twenty guys pumping iron. He suspected they were all on the football team, and that not a single one of them would rally to his side if this guy started to get rough. He knew instantly the guy was looking for a fight. He had an instinct for such things.

"It's not bad," he muttered, letting go of the bars and sitting up. Perhaps if he went on to another machine, he thought, there was a chance the guy would leave him alone. Unfortunately, the guy was blocking his way.

"What did you say, boy?" the big white kid asked.

"Nothing."

"Yeah, you did. I heard you say something. What was it?"

Nick scooted back to where he was able to swing his leg around the bench press table without touching the guy. "I said, it was not bad. The weight wasn't."

The guy smiled. A couple of his buddies behind him stopped lifting to watch. "You must be pretty strong, boy. How many pounds were you lifting there?"

"I don't know."

"You don't know? How come you don't know?"

Nick stood up. "I wasn't keeping track."

The guy followed him to the next machine, which exercised the hamstrings. To use it, Nick would have to lie face down, which was not something he wanted to do at the moment. He stood undecided as all around him more guys stopped working out to stare.

"What are you waiting for?" the dude asked, moving closer. Nick estimated the guy had forty pounds on him, but knew that his gut was soft, a swift fist in the diaphragm and the white kid would go down. Nick also estimated that about twenty guys would jump him the moment the guy hit the floor.

"Nothing." Nick had never mastered the art of talking his way out of a fight.

"Aren't our machines good enough for you?"

Nick lowered his head. "They're all right."

"Just all right? You sure spend enough time on them, time that someone else on the team could be using. Are you getting my meaning, boy?"

Nick got it very well. But suddenly he didn't feel that he should. This is how it had always been with him. He would try to avoid a confrontation up to a point—and then he just wouldn't bend anymore. He would explode. He hated being called boy.

"No."

The guy lost his smile. "No what?"

Nick looked him straight in the eye. He hadn't really looked anyone in the eye all week. "I have as much right to use this equipment as you do. If you think I don't, that's your problem."

"Really? Well, I think it just became your problem." And with that, the guy shoved him hard in the chest.

Nick had been expecting the move, and it was still his intention to floor the guy without seriously injuring him. But what followed proved unexpected. Absorbing the blow without losing his balance, Nick moved slightly to the right and forward. He planned to grab the guy by the left arm, spin him around, and put him in a choke hold. He figured that would be the best way to keep his teammates at bay. He couldn't believe it when the overweight tub anticipated *his* move and caught his right hand, whipping him into the nearby wall with incredible force. On the wall hung a mirror the guys used to admire themselves. It splintered on impact beneath Nick's skull, cutting into his scalp. Then he was on the floor, trying to stand. Blood trickled down the side of his face. The guy's feet were approaching.

"You goddamn piece of—" the dude swore as he let fly a kick toward Nick's forehead. Nick was through treating him carefully. He ducked the fat foot and crouched, coiling the power of his legs. The momentum of the misplaced kick left the white dude twisted at an awkward angle. Nick launched himself upward, grabbing the guy's hair with both hands and snapping his right knee into his groin. The bastard couldn't even scream out. Doubling up, making a strangled gasping sound, he fell to the floor, turning a sick pasty color.

"Who's next?" Nick barked, glaring at the remainder of the room. He doubted that he'd scare off the whole gang, and he was right. You couldn't bluff people out of a twenty-to-one advantage. A few of the stockier fellows began to close in. Instinctively, Nick knelt and grabbed ahold of a large jagged slice of mirror. The players paused warily, glancing at one another. It was then that the head of the football team, Coach Campbell, barged in.

Nick had seen the man before. Approximately forty years old, he had tan leathery skin and a wide blunt face Nick thought particularly ugly. Although below average in height, he was built like a tree trunk and had one of those thick raspy voices that was usually the result of years of shouting.

"What's going on here?" he demanded. He saw his

41

player rolled up on the floor and then saw Nick bleeding, with the glass knife in his hand. A look of pure disgust filled his already disgusting face. "Put that down!"

Nick set the piece of mirror on the floor. He had been gripping it so hard, it had cut into his fingers, and they were bleeding as well. Coach Campbell moved so close to Nick that Nick could feel his hot breath on his bare chest. "What did you do to Gordon?" he asked.

"He attacked m-me," Nick stuttered.

"He attacked *you?* Why would he attack someone carrying a knife?" The coach backed off a step, scowled down at Gordon. "Skater, Fields, help The Rock to the infirmary."

The Rock, Nick thought.

The players did as told and soon the guy had been cleared away. From the outside, Nick knew he was standing perfectly still, but inside he was shaking. He half expected the coach to belt him in the face. Worse, he had no doubt at all that he was to be expelled, and that his father would kick him out of the house when he heard.

"What's your name, son?" Coach Campbell asked.

"Nick Grutler."

"Where you from? What are you doing here?"

"This is where I go to school."

"Who gave you permission to use the facilities in this room?"

"The other coach."

"Who?"

"I don't remember his name."

Coach Campbell folded his arms across his chest, nodding to himself. "I know who you are. You're that transfer from Pontiac High downtown. I was warned about you. I see I should have listened."

Nick swallowed. "He started it."

Coach Campbell looked around the room. "Is this true?" He waited for an answer. No one spoke up. The coach sighed, shook his head. "Grutler, either you're a liar or else no one here gives a damn about your hide. I don't know which is worse. But I can tell you one thing, you're on your way out, out of this room and off this campus." He began to walk away. "See someone at the infirmary about your cuts. Then come to my office."

A heavy weight descended on Nick, and for the first time an outsider might have noticed a crack in his reserve. He was stooped over slightly; he couldn't quite catch his breath. He really had wanted to fit in.

Then the unexpected happened for the second time in a few minutes. One of the guys in the corner began to laugh. The sound caused Coach Campbell to stop in the doorway and glance over his shoulder. The guy in the corner kept right on laughing, louder and louder. The coach turned toward him, glaring.

"What are you giggling about, Desmond?" Coach Campbell demanded.

The guy got up slowly, shaking his head. "It's just that you remind me, Coach, of a sheriff in a movie I saw last night on TV. The sheriff tried to put a black fella behind bars just 'cause he didn't like his looks. Sitting here, I was thinking you talked just like him. You see that movie, Coach? You would have liked it. The sheriff ended up going to jail."

"What's your point?"

The guy yawned. "Seems to me if The Rock wants to pick on people that can kick his ass, I don't see why it's anybody's business except his and the guy he's hassling."

"Are you saying The Rock started this? Why didn't you speak up earlier?"

"Couldn't be bothered, I guess."

Coach Campbell glanced at Nick, then back at the guy. Nick could see Desmond was no slouch, either. About six feet with a head of thick brown hair, he had a powerfully developed physique. More important to Nick, though, when he had begun to laugh, the other guys in the room had backed off slightly, as though even his humor intimidated them. Coach Campbell seemed to take him seriously enough.

"What are you doing in here, anyway, Desmond?" the coach asked. "Don't you have a cross-country race to run this afternoon?"

"I do, yeah. So what?"

"You shouldn't be tiring yourself out beforehand lifting weights." Then his tone took on a bitter edge. "You shouldn't be running at all. Why don't you suit up for tonight's game? We need some help at full-back."

"I'll tell you why, Coach. 'Cause I don't feel like it."

"You're wasting God-given talents. You could go to college on a scholarship. You have the potential to go to Notre Dame!"

Desmond looked bored, sat down. "No way, I ain't even Catholic."

Coach Campbell let out an exasperated breath, turned to Nick. "All right, Grutler, we'll let it pass this time. But in the future, try to stay out of trouble."

Nick had not expected an apology. "Yeah, sure."

When the coach had left, everyone went back to pumping iron, except for Desmond, who pulled on a torn cross-country jersey and strolled outside. Nick caught up with him on the hot asphalt between the weight room and the gym.

"Hey, I just wanted to thank you," Nick said.

The guy didn't even slow down. "No problem. I got a real kick out of seeing you knee The Rock between the legs. I bet that pig can't stand up straight for a week."

"Well, I won't forget it. I owe you one."

"You don't owe me nothing. But if you want to buy me a case of beer someday, I'll drink it."

And with that, Desmond walked away.

Nick did not go to the infirmary. He didn't know where it was, and he didn't want to run into The Rock and his pals if he *was* able to find it. He took a shower instead and afterward held a wad of toilet paper to the cut on his scalp. Eventually the bleeding began to subside. The resulting scar would be hidden under his hair, but because he had hit the mirror with the side of his head, and not the back, the flesh between his left temple and left eye had also begun to swell. He worried what his father would say when he saw it. His father had a violent temper.

Besides having given him walking orders to stay out of trouble, his father had also told him not to come home that afternoon without a job. Nick had figured his best bet would be the nearby mall. He knew roughly where it was and thought he might be able to walk there in less than an hour. He'd worked before, in his old neighborhood, loading freight at the docks. He wondered if the stores in the mall would want him to fill out all kinds of papers before letting him show what he could do. He hoped not.

Before he set out for the mall, he stopped at the soda machines in the courtyard. He was disappointed to discover he didn't have enough money to buy a Coke. He was standing there, fishing through his pockets for a possible hidden dime, when a small Hispanic girl came up at his side.

"May I?" she asked. He was blocking her way. He stepped aside hastily.

"I don't have the right change," he mumbled. He'd seen the girl before, at lunch, sitting by herself beneath a tree hugging her knees. She had long black hair tied back in a ponytail that reached to her waist.

"Oh." She put in her change, made her selection. A can of orange soda popped out below. "What do you need?"

"Nothing, I wasn't that thirsty." He was dying for a drink. "Thanks, anyway."

"No," she said, glancing up at him with big, lustrous eyes, a serious, perhaps sad, expression. "I have change."

Nick shrugged. "I need a quarter."

She reached in her tiny purse. "I have three dimes."

He took out his dime and three nickels. This was all the money he had in the world. He'd gone without lunch. This was another reason he needed a job in a hurry. He had to buy almost all his own food. He took her dimes and bought his Coke, giving her back the spare nickel. "Thanks," he said, opening the can, shifting nervously on his feet. She was staring at him.

"Do you know you're bleeding?" she asked finally.

He touched the side of his head. It had started again. "It's nothing. I cut it."

"Does it hurt?"

"No. A little. It will stop in a minute."

She went to touch the area. He recoiled automatically, and she quickly withdrew her hand. "I'm sorry," she said.

"It's really nothing," he said quickly.

"You were in a fight, weren't you?"

He began to shake his head, stopped. "Yes, I was."

Her next question caught him off guard. "Did you win?"

"I don't think he'll want to fight me again."

She offered her hand. "I'm Maria Gonzales. You're Nick, aren't you?"

He shook her hand briefly. Her skin was cool, very soft. "How did you know?"

"I've watched you this week. You walk from one place to another. You never talk to anyone. I did that when I first got here."

She had a strong Spanish accent. He wondered if she had only recently come into the United States. He'd had experience with a variety of ethnic groups in his old neighborhood. He suspected she wasn't from Mexico, but from farther south, from El Salvador or Nicaragua. "I don't know many people here," he said.

"Do you know anybody?"

"I know the name of the guy who threw me into the mirror."

She smiled faintly. She had deep red heart-shaped lips, smooth high cheeks untouched by makeup. Her pink dress hung loose and cool but he could tell she had a fine figure. She had a freshness about her he had seldom seen in his old neighborhood. She had probably led a clean life.

"And I bet he knows your name," she said.

Nick smiled, too, pleased with himself for having made a mildly funny remark, and happy to be talking to someone who was kind. Yet at the same time he felt the sudden urge to curtail the conversation. Perhaps he wanted to quit while he was ahead. Maybe he didn't think he was good enough to be talking to someone like Maria.

"Nice meeting you," he mumbled, backing up a step. "I better be going."

"Do you take the bus home?"

"No."

"Oh, you have a car?"

He stopped. The truth sounded so poor. "Not really."

"Where do you live?"

In a shack.

"Near Houston and Second."

"I live over that way. You don't walk home every day, do you?"

"Sometimes I hitch a ride." No one had picked him up so far.

"You should take the bus. There's one coming in about ten minutes. You shouldn't be walking home after getting hit like that on the head."

The urge to get away intensified. He felt exposed, as though any second this girl was going to see something repulsive in him. He took another step back. "I'll be all right. I've got to go. Thanks again for the Coke."

"Take care of yourself, Nick."

He hurried off the campus, walking in the direction of the mall. He didn't understand it. She had sounded concerned about him.

CHAPTER FOUR

Sara Cantrell approached the soda machines seconds after Maria Gonzales and Nick Grutler finished talking. Sara was feeling pretty good. She was glad she had spoken her mind about the candidates in the assembly that afternoon. The whole country was in love with phonies, she felt. The bimboes on sitcoms, the rock dopers on MTV, the rich liars in D.C. It made her sick just going into the supermarket and having to look at all those fakes on the covers of *People* magazine. One day she'd like to start a magazine of her own where she could interview people like herself, people who knew it was all a big joke.

Sara had a bad thirst. But when she put her quarters in the soda machine and punched the 7-Up button, nothing happened. She tried the other buttons, then the coin return, and still nothing happened. Her good mood went right out the window. Those were the only two quarters she had! What did this stupid machine expect her to do, drink water? She pounded it with her fists, kicked it with her feet. Her quarters must be stuck.

49

The administration's probably behind this. Trying to weasel extra money out of us kids to buy themselves magazines for their goddamn lounge.

She remembered a move a guy had done on one of the soda machines at lunch. He had grabbed ahold of it with both hands and tilted it slightly on edge, coughing up not only his money but a couple of free cans as well. Setting down her books, she stretched out her arms, trying to get a grip on it. She was not a big girl, nor was she particularly strong. Nevertheless, when she tilted the machine to the right, she was surprised to see it rock right out of her hands. It hit the asphalt with an incredible bang, causing her to jump. Taking a quick look around to make sure no one had seen her, she collected her books and hurried toward the front of the campus. At Mesa High she'd never once had a soda machine fall over on her. This was a stupid school.

Sara was supposed to meet Polly and Jessica in the parking lot directly across from campus. They had been forced to put their cars there; Tabb's lot was filled. Sara was temporarily without wheels. Her dad had taken them away when she had received her third ticket in a month for running a red light. It was a real drag—and totally unfair. She had only gone through the lights after stopping and looking both ways. Why, she thought, should she have to sit and wait on a mechanism that didn't care if she crossed the road or not?

Her dad didn't know she had picked up Jessica and her folks at three in the morning. She'd run half a dozen red lights driving to the airport.

A row of bushes separated the school from the sidewalk that ran along its west side. They were tall, thick shrubs, and putting one foot onto the sidewalk,

Sara couldn't see more than a few yards in either direction. She didn't even hear Russ Desmond coming.

When he hit her, she hardly felt a thing. One second she was walking, the next, flying. She must have closed her eyes. When she opened them, she was sitting in the bushes with a branch running up her pant leg and a flower stuck in her ear.

"Oh, wow," she breathed. A guy with the greatest set of legs she had ever seen was standing over her breathing hard.

"You all right?" he asked.

"What happened?"

"You got in my way."

"Really?" Did this guy throw every chick that got in his way into the bushes? She sat up with effort, a muscle in her lower back protesting. The guy grabbed her arm and pulled her onto the sidewalk as if she were light as a feather. The second he let go of her, she reeled backward. The sidewalk wobbled under her feet. "Thanks a whole bunch," she muttered, blinking. "Who the hell are you?"

"Russ Desmond." He wiped his sweaty face on his arm, still panting like a dog. "You've got leaves in your hair."

"I didn't grow them, believe me." She tried to brush them away and poked herself in the ear. Her hands were trembling. Maybe she had a concussion or something. The guy looked pretty far-out, like a biker in a track uniform. "I'm Sara Cantrell. You must have seen me at lunch."

"Huh?"

Just then a multicolored herd of various-shaped teenage boys came storming down the sidewalk. They had appeared from around a corner, and there was only a second to get out of their way. Russ Desmond watched them pass without a great deal of interest.

"Do the guys migrate at Tabb or what?" she asked, getting back down from the steps where she had run for safety.

"We're just having a little race is all. What did you mean, I must have seen you at lunch? What happened at lunch?"

It hit Sara then what was going. "Wait a sec, you're in the middle of a race?"

"That's what I just said."

"No, I mean, *you're* in the race?"

"Yeah."

"But you were winning!" She looked down the sidewalk in the direction of the rapidly vanishing group of cross-country runners. "Get going. Go after them. Hurry!"

"I will," he said, sounding vaguely annoyed. "In a minute. I just want to make sure you're all right."

"I'm all right. Get out of here."

"First tell me what happened at lunch?"

"I gave a speech. Didn't you hear my speech? It doesn't matter. I'm sure someone taped it. You can listen to it after your race. Now get out of here. Go. Scoot. Good-bye."

He nodded, gave a quick smile. "You've wrecked my time, Sara."

Watching him run off, pulling leaves from her hair, she muttered, "Well, you wrecked my makeup, Russ."

Russ Desmond.

Polly and Jessica showed up a few minutes later. They were talking about Alice's party, or rather, arguing about it. Sara loved arguments. She hated to simply discuss things.

"Food doesn't have to be a big deal," Jessica was saying. "We don't have to feed everyone dinner for god's sake. All we need are a few sweet and salty dishes, and plenty to drink. Isn't that right, Sara?"

"That is true."

"But people are going to be showing up with beer," Polly said. "You remember what happened at Alice's last party? Claudia Philips got drunk and threw up all over Kirk Holden."

"So we won't invite Claudia," Jessica said.

"Or Kirk," Sara added.

"And we can put on the invitations that no alcohol will be allowed," Jessica said.

Polly grimaced. "We have to print up invitations?"

"Of course," Sara said. "We have to show these barbarians we have class."

"Who's going to pay for all this?" Polly asked. "Me?"

"No, of course not," Sara said. "Alice will."

"Alice has the same account as I do," Polly complained. Then she paused, staring at Sara. "What happened to you? You have leaves in your hair, Sara."

"Well, you have a fat ass, Polly. And this evening I'll wash my hair and look just wonderful, and you'll still have a fat ass."

"You wouldn't look wonderful if a car full of plastic surgeons ran over you on the freeway," Polly retorted.

Sara wrinkled her nose. "Huh?"

"Stop it, you two," Jessica said. They had reached Jessica's and Polly's cars. Jessica had a Toyota; Polly, a Mercedes. Both cars were brand-new. Sara had had a nice car once, before she had run into a stupid telephone pole. Jessica continued, "We have to decide whether we want to make it a swimming party or not. What do you think, Sara?"

"Definitely. We can go skinny-dipping."

"We're not going skinny-dipping," Polly said. "It's against the law."

"Only when you've got a fat—" Sara stopped, looking around. "Where's Alice?"

Jessica and Polly glanced at each other. "She went home early," Jessica said.

"What's the matter?" Sara asked. "Does she have cramps?"

Polly hesitated. "Yeah."

"That's a shame," Sara said. She liked having Alice around. That girl could take an insult better than anybody; she always just laughed.

Jessica yawned. "Let's talk about this later, at the game. I've got to take a nap now or I'm going to turn into a pumpkin." She opened her car door. "You want Polly or me to take you home, Sara?"

"I'll go with you."

"I can drive us to the game," Polly said eagerly.

"Whatever," Jessica nodded, still yawning. "Get in, Sara."

When they were cruising down the road, the air conditioner on full and Polly following on their tail, Sara asked, "Why are you going to the game? You should stay home and rest."

Jessica rubbed her tired eyes beneath her glasses. She had only put on the glasses at Sara's insistence. Lately Jessica's sight had gotten so bad that Sara hated to get in the car when she was driving. That morning in political science, before she fell asleep, Sara had noticed Jessica straining to see the screen. The girl had a history of allergies; her eyes were too sensitive for contacts, even for soft lenses. Yet she resisted wearing her glasses, even when there was no one else around; simple vanity, there was no question about it.

"I would, but I told my journalism teacher I'd take some pictures for the paper," Jessica said.

"You volunteered?"

"Not exactly. The teacher saw the pictures I'd taken last year for Mesa's annual. She likes my work. I think she's been waiting for me and my camera to show up. I don't mind. I've got to do something now that I'm not a cheerleader anymore. And I promised Alice I'd come. She has this guy she wants me to meet."

"What's his name?"

"I don't know."

"Bill Skater?"

Jessica smiled. "I wish. It'll be fun watching him play tonight."

"It might be *funny*. I wasn't kidding in the assembly when I said I'd heard he was awful."

Jessica shrugged. "I could care less what he can do with a football."

Sara sneered. "What makes you think you're ever going to find out what he can do with you?"

Jessica grinned. "It's only September. I've got till June. I'm going to invite him to the party."

"I know."

Jessica lost her grin. "You don't think we're pressuring Polly into something she doesn't want to do, do you?"

"Polly's just being Polly. If we didn't give her a shove every now and then, she'd be mummified in her bedroom closet. Besides, the party was Alice's idea." Sara rubbed her aching arm. A purple bruise was beginning to appear below her elbow. "I have someone I'm going to invite, too."

"Who?"

"This guy I ran into."

CHAPTER FIVE

Michael Olson was doing inventory at the 7-Eleven when Nick Grutler walked in. Michael had seen Nick at school—it was hard not to see that tall, black body—and wondered if he played basketball. He had thought of asking him. It was not fear of Nick that had kept Michael quiet. Once Bubba had accused Michael of being especially kind to minorities because he felt guilty about not fully trusting them. It was Bubba's contention that everyone was prejudiced to a degree, and the best anyone could do was to try not to let it interfere with how he treated other races. But Michael was genuinely color blind. People were people to him.

Michael had not approached Nick because Nick did not look as if he wanted to be approached. It was as simple as that. The Rock probably wished he'd had as keen instincts. Michael had heard what had happened in the weight room. But unlike Russ Desmond, he did not take pleasure in The Rock's downfall. Michael disliked violence in any form.

But now that Nick had come into his store, Michael felt no qualms about introducing himself. He nodded as Nick approached the counter. "Hi, how are you doing? Don't we go to school together?"

A flicker of surprise crossed Nick's eyes. "I go to Tabb," he mumbled.

"So do I." Michael offered his hand. "I'm Michael Olson. Nick Grutler, right?"

Nick shook his hand. He had a mean grip. "How did you know?"

"You can expect most people at school to know your name after you floored The Rock."

A note of wariness entered his voice. "Was he a friend of yours?"

"The Rock doesn't have many friends." Michael had only brought up the weight room incident because he wanted to answer Nick's question honestly. He wanted to get off the subject. "You look like you've been out in the sun all afternoon. Can I get you something to drink? You know we sell soft drinks in glasses here as well as bottles and cans." Michael picked up the king-size cup behind him. "These are only fifty-five cents."

Nick looked vaguely uncomfortable. He pulled a couple of silver dollars out of his pocket and laid them on the counter. "These are good, aren't they?"

Michael picked one up. "Yeah, sure. Though you don't see many of them around. Did you get them at the bank?"

"No. At the Italian market."

"In the mall? Man, I love the smell in that place."

"Their warehouse in the back don't smell so good."

"What were you doing back there?"

"They needed some boxes moved."

Michael knew the owner of the market. He had probably worked Nick to death for a couple of hours and then given him the two silver dollars, probably thinking Nick would imagine they were worth more or something.

Michael was looking for a new employee. The owners had told him to hire whomever he wanted. They trusted his judgment.

"Was it a temporary job?" he asked, knowing it was. Who would hire a black with bloody hair?

"Yeah. I'll have one of those big Cokes for fifty-five cents."

"Sure." Michael reached over, scooped some ice into the paper cup. "Have you done enough work for one day?"

Nick seemed interested. "I could do more."

"I'm rearranging our storeroom. But because I have to keep coming back up front to handle the register, it's taking me forever. It's back-breaking work—all you're doing is lifting—but someone like you could probably finish most of it in a few hours. I could give you thirty bucks under the table, no tax taken out?"

Nick accepted his Coke, took a deep swallow. "Show me where to start."

Michael led Nick to the rear of the store and gave him an overview of how disorganized things were. Nick grasped immediately what had to be done. After a couple minutes of discussion, Michael left Nick alone. He needed help with the storeroom, true, but Michael was also using the chore as a test. If Nick did good work, he would offer him a permanent part-time job. It would be handy having someone around who could reach the top shelves without a ladder.

Two hours later, as it began to get dark outside and the faint sounds of Tabb High's band drifted through the open door from the direction of the school stadium, Nick reappeared and announced he had finished. One look in the back and Michael was astounded. Not only was everything neatly arranged,

Nick had obviously used his own initiative—and used it wisely—in setting up certain sections. This meant a lot to Michael. He'd previously had a couple of employees who had been fine workers except that they had required constant supervision. Obviously Nick had common sense as well as powerful biceps.

Getting three tens out of the cash register, Michael made his offer. He could guarantee him at least twenty hours a week, although some weeks he'd need Nick close to thirty. He gave him a brief summary of what his responsibilities would be, and what he would start at. Nick listened patiently, and from his stoic expression, it was impossible to tell what was going on in his head. He asked only two questions.

"Will I be working with you all the time?"

"Most of the time," Michael said.

Nick thought for a moment. "Why are you doing this for me?"

"I'm offering you the job because you've proven to me you know how to work. I'm not *doing* anything for you."

Nick nodded. "I appreciate it, anyway. The only one who would even talk to me at the mall was that Italian guy, and I know he just ripped me off." He put his thirty dollars in his pocket. "Can I just keep working now?"

Michael smiled. "You'll take it then?"

Nick smiled, too, finally letting his pleasure show. "Yeah. But I'll have to call my dad to tell him I've got a job."

Michael pulled the phone from beneath the counter. "Sure, then take a break. There's a lot to do here, but you don't have to kill yourself."

A half hour later Michael wondered if he'd lied to Nick about not killing himself. They got held up by a guy with a gun.

Nick was in the cooler, putting the beverages in from behind, and Michael had returned to the inventory report and the register when the masked man entered. He wore a dark nylon stocking over his head on top of a blue knitted cap and a pair of silver sunglasses. He had his gun drawn as he entered.

"Get your hands up!" he snapped, waving his revolver nervously. Michael carefully set down his note board and pen. His first reaction was not one of fear, but of pure amazement. It was only eight-thirty. Who would be stupid enough to try to pull off a holdup now, when anybody could walk in at any second? The 7-Eleven was open twenty-four hours a day, for god's sake. But Michael didn't consider suggesting to the guy he come back later.

"What can I do for you?" he asked calmly, slowly raising his hands. There was a button located beneath the counter that would sound an alarm at the local police station. Unfortunately, it was so situated that Michael would have to ask permission of any thief to use it. The clink of bottles continued to sound from behind the cooler. Nick must not know they had uninvited company.

"What's that?" the fellow demanded. He wasn't very good at this. Outside of his obvious anxiety, he had a rather squeaky voice. Shifting the gun from one hand to the other, he scratched under his nylon stocking.

"What was what?" Michael asked.

"Do you have someone back there?" He peered toward the cooler. It must have been hard to see through the disguise. "Hey, you back there! Get out here before I blow your buddy away!"

"Yeah, come out here, Nick. We've got a guest."

Nick appeared a moment later, his arms hanging by his sides. "Mike?"

"It's nothing to worry about," Michael said, trying to relax everybody concerned. "We're all cool here, aren't we?"

"Yeah, it's cool," the guy spat out, cocking his revolver. "Give me your goddamn money. No funny business." He gestured toward Nick. "And you, get your hands up and come over here."

Michael did not want to give him the money. In no way did he plan on risking his or Nick's life to save it, but he did feel a responsibility to the owners of the store to get to the alarm button if at all possible. Opening the register, he rapidly began to toss all the change on the counter, like he was scared and didn't know what he was doing. The masked man shook his gun angrily.

"Just the bills, man! Just the bills!"

"Yes, sir, the bills," Michael answered breathlessly, pulling the drawer out still farther, past the point of no return. The drawer slipped from the register, the money pouring loudly onto the floor. Michael feigned shock. "Wow, I'm sorry." He bent over. "Here, I'll pick it up."

"Man, you're a peach." The masked man chuckled, falling for Michael's chicken act, leaning forward to watch him better. But it was already too late. Michael had hit the button the instant he had crouched down. At this very second, several patrol cars would be changing direction and moving toward them.

Michael didn't know when he had hired Nick that Nick had never depended on a cop for anything in his life. He didn't know about Nick's incredible reflexes.

As Michael began to collect the money behind the counter, Nick lashed out with his foot at the gun, sending it ricocheting off the ceiling and into the cereal row. Startled, the masked man twisted around to retrieve it. Before he could get halfway there, Nick

61

grabbed ahold of his arm and whipped him into a stack of beer bottles. The guy slid toward the freezer on a wave of broken glass, foam, and noise.

"Oh, God," Michael whispered. Moving quickly, Nick collected the gun and turned on the fallen thief. Seeing him coming, the guy frantically began to rip at the nylon over his face.

"Mike, don't let him kill me!" he cried. "It's me! It's Kats!"

"Kats," Michael said, disgusted. "I should have known."

Carl Barber, better known as Kats, was a nineteen-year-old loser. He had gone to Tabb High for five years, taken advanced pottery and Shop I, II, and III, and still hadn't graduated. He'd had a life-long dream of joining the marines, but without the diploma, they wouldn't take him. He worked at the gas station up the street from Tabb High. He had oil under his fingernails a surgeon couldn't have removed. Whenever kids from the school drove into the station—dozens of students cruised by every morning and afternoon—Kats got into a fight with them. Admittedly, Kats usually didn't start the fights. He was one of those rare people that *no* one respected. Guys would pull into the full-service area and tell him to dust their tires. According to Bubba—who took Kats about as seriously as everyone else but who nevertheless spent a fair amount of time in his company—Kats had been genetically cloned from Rodney Dangerfield. Nothing ever went his way, that was for sure.

"Stop, Nick," Michael said. "I know this guy."

Nick looked bewildered. He shook the weapon in his hand. "This is real, Mike. He was pointing it right at us."

Michael came from behind the counter, furious. "So

62

you hold us up with a real gun! What the hell do you think you're doing?''

Kats grinned, his ugly teeth protruding from beneath his thin black mustache. It was not true, like some said, that he greased his hair and mustache with oil from the gas station, at least not intentionally. But it was a fact he was always running his hands through his hair even when he was laboring beneath filthy dripping heaps.

"I was just trying to give you boys a little scare." Kats giggled. "I did, too. I saw the way you fumbled that cash register!"

Michael turned to Nick. "All right, go ahead and waste him."

"Mike!" Kats cried, squirming in a pond of Miller Lite.

Michael took a step closer. "I fumbled the drawer on purpose! I hit a button to call the police. It also trips an alarm in the homes of the owners. They're all going to be here in minutes. What am I supposed to tell them?"

Kats tried to get up without cutting himself, brushing off scraps of glass knit together with torn beer labels. "Christ, Mike, what's the big deal? The gun wasn't loaded. It was just a prank." He grinned again. Michael really wished he would stop. "How'd you like my disguise? I knew you wouldn't recognize me with that voice I was using. Got it off an old gangster movie I watched last night. What do you think of my piece, huh? Picked it up at the swap meet last Saturday. It fires a twenty-two—"

"Shut up," Michael said wearily. "Just take your piece and get out of here before the police arrive. I don't know what I'm going to tell them." He tried to count the broken bottles. "But I do know one thing, you're paying for this mess."

Kats tried to snap the revolver from Nick's hands, failed. Nick did not appear to trust Kats any more now than when Kats had been holding them at gunpoint. Nick gave the weapon to Michael, instead, who accepted it reluctantly. Michael had never understood why anyone made handguns. They were no good for hunting. They were only good for killing people. Had Kats been stowing it in his refrigerator, he wondered. The steel felt unreasonably cold in his hand. He was anxious to be rid of it.

"Why should I?" Kats said angrily. "It was this big lug here who tripped me. I ain't paying for it, no way."

"If you don't," Michael said flatly, "I'll give the police your address."

Kats saw he was serious, nodded. "OK, lighten up. I'll pay for the beer. And I'll leave now." He started toward the door.

"Go out the back," Michael said. "I don't want some cop taking a shot at you." He held out the gun. "Take this with you."

Kats smiled as he accepted the revolver, slipping it into his belt beneath his shirt. He had a fetish for guns. It was probably part of the reason he wanted to join the marines. His crummy single-room apartment was packed with rifles, shotguns, all kinds of ammunition. "Good thinking. Hey, you're not really mad at me, are you, Mike? You know I would never try to rob you. You and me, we go way back. Coming to the game later?"

"Yeah, maybe." Michael chuckled in spite of himself. This was turning out to be a weird day. "Go ahead, get out of here. Go home and take a shower. You stink."

"Thanks, Mike. See you later."

When he was gone, Michael called the police. Turned out they had received no alarm. He called one of his bosses, told him he had accidentally bumped the button. The boss gave him the same story as the police; no alarm had gone off. Hanging up the phone, Michael pulled on the wiring attached to the button. It was burned out, shorted.

"At least now we've got your feet to protect us," he told Nick. "That is, if you haven't changed your mind and want to quit?"

"I'm not quitting, Mike. I'm just beginning to feel at home."

Between the two of them, they cleaned up the mess. The equivalent of three cases had been destroyed. Michael decided to juggle the numbers on the store inventory until Kats came up with the money, if he ever did. Michael figured he'd probably end up paying for the damage out of his own pocket.

Michael's replacement, the twenty-year-old son of one of the bosses, came in at nine o'clock. Amir went full-time to the local junior college and spent most nights at the store. As a result, he was chronically exhausted, and did little during the wee hours of the morning except run the cash register and study. He simply nodded when Michael introduced Nick as their new employee. Michael hoped Amir's father had the same reaction.

Michael and Nick were walking out the front doors of the 7-Eleven when the phone rang. An hour had passed since the phony holdup. It was Bubba. Michael took the call in the small office in the back.

"Did you invite Nick Grutler to come to the game with us?" Bubba asked.

"Yeah." The invitation had surprised Nick, but he had accepted without hesitation. He seemed to be looking forward to it. "Where are you? You said you'd pick me up at nine."

"Kats is here," Bubba said, lowering his voice. "He tells me Grutler tried to kill him."

"Did Kats also tell you that he pulled a gun on us?"

"Yeah, but that was a joke, Mike. What's wrong with this guy? I hear he practically cut The Rock's throat this afternoon."

"Get off it, Bubba. You know as well as I, The Rock started it. Nick's cool. Are you going to pick us up or not?"

"If it was just up to me, I'd be there already. But Kats wants to go to the game, and he says if Nick comes with us, things might get ugly. He's full of it, I know, but why don't you and Nick go on alone?"

"Since when does Kats tell you what to do?"

"It's no big deal. Let's not fight about it. I'll meet you there. Come on, it's getting late, and I want to talk to Clair before halftime ends."

Michael was disappointed in his friend. "Whatever you say, Bubba."

Michael owned his own car, an off-white Toyota that had had over a hundred thousand miles on it when he bought it. The interior was clean, and although the engine drank a quart of oil every month, it ran smoothly. Yet as he opened the passenger door and adjusted the seat for Nick's long legs, Michael thought how plain it would look to a girl like Jessica Hart who had just returned from sunbathing in the Aegean Sea. He was hoping to see her at the game, maybe say hello.

The school lot was packed; they had to park a block away in a residential area. Walking toward the stadium, Michael caught a glimpse of the scoreboard: Tabb High 0; Visitors 6. The marching bands and drill teams had taken the field. The snack bar was beset with thick lines. They had definitely made it for halftime.

66

"Have you ever played any sports?" Michael asked Nick as they hurried up the steps that led to the entrance.

"Nope."

"How about some pickup basketball games?"

"Oh, yeah, we used to play those." Nick chuckled. "But we never followed many rules. You had to knock a guy unconscious for a foul to be called."

"Have you ever thought of going out for the team here?"

Nick looked uncomfortable. "I don't think I'd fit in on a team." He reached for his back pocket. "How much is it to get in?"

"When you're this late, it's free."

Once inside the gate, they both caught a whiff of the hot dogs and decided they were starving. Nick insisted it would be his treat and went to wait in line while Michael made a quick stop at the rest room. He was heading back to the snack bar when he ran into Alice McCoy. She had a guy with her, a thin redhead who was literally dragging her toward the exit.

"Mikey!" she called, disengaging herself from her date and running to give him a quick hug. "Where have you been? I've been looking for you all night. Remember, I wanted you to meet my friend?"

"Well, I'm here now," he said cheerfully.

She glanced back over her shoulder. Her date had turned away, staring into the brick wall behind the snack bar. Alice smiled quickly, nervously. "Did you have to work late?"

"No later than usual. Do you have to leave now?"

"Yeah. We—we have to go somewhere."

"That's too bad. I can always meet your friend another time."

"No, I want to be there when you meet her." Again, she glanced at her date, obviously trying to come to

67

some sort of decision. Michael nodded toward the guy.

"Is that your new boyfriend?"

She didn't seem to hear him. "Could you stay here a sec?"

"Sure."

Alice walked back to the guy, spoke softly to him. First he shook his head. But as Alice persisted, he shrugged, pulling out a comb and running it through his long, thin red hair. Touching him gratefully on the arm, Alice returned to Michael.

"I'll go get her," she said. "Stay here, right here. OK?"

"All right." Watching her disappear into the crowd, Michael wondered why Alice had not introduced him to her date. Ordinarily she was extremely polite. Something about the way the guy stood, his hands plowed into his pockets, completely ignoring everyone around him, disturbed Michael. He decided he'd introduce himself.

"Hi, I'm Michael Olson," he said, walking up and offering his hand. "I'm a friend of Alice's. You're Clark, right?"

The guy had the brightest green eyes Michael had ever seen. They practically glowed in the dark. His gaze lingered on Michael's outstretched hand for a moment before he lazily shook it.

"I suppose," he said. He had a deep southern accent, a disconcerting stare. His black leather biker jacket hung loose over his shoulders; Michael suspected there was nothing but skin and bone beneath it. The guy needed to see a doctor. His palm was warm and clammy.

"Alice tells me you're also an artist?"

Clark found the comparison amusing. "She loves pretty colors. I like sharp lines, black and white."

"Huh. What's that mean?"

"That I'm unique."

What does she see in him?

The question made Michael pause and consider how well he knew Alice. From day one, he'd neatly classified her as a carefree darling. He should know better by now that no one was that neat, or that unique.

"She told me you've had a big influence on her work?" he asked.

"She's talked about me?"

"On occasion."

"Alice doesn't work. Alice's got too much money to work. Alice's got too many dresses." He grinned suddenly. "Do you like the dress she's wearing tonight? I like when her sister wears it. It looks a lot different on Polly."

Michael had met Polly once. Alice had brought her by his store last spring. He assumed Clark was making a lewd reference to her large breasts. His dislike for the guy deepened. "Where are you from?" he asked.

Clark lost his grin. "Why?"

"I was just wondering, that's all. Do you go to school around here?"

"No."

"Where do you go?"

"The other side of town." Clark's gaze wandered toward the playing field. "Our team's as lousy as yours. But in our stadium, you can always lean your head back and look at the trees in the sky."

Michael frowned. "I don't mean to be rude, but are you stoned?" He was worried about Alice driving home in the car with him.

"I'm here man, right here." Clark yawned, turning again to face the wall behind the snack bar. "Alice had better get back soon. I've got to get out of here."

"Why?"

Bubba and Kats appeared. Since Clark had not bothered to answer his last question, Michael felt under no obligation to introduce him to them. Bubba had on a black suede jacket, a red handkerchief tucked in the pocket, a white silk shirt underneath. Kats was no longer dripping but still stunk of beer. Bubba had probably thrown Kats's clothes in the dryer without washing them. Clark continued to stare at the wall. It didn't even have graffiti on it. Michael allowed Bubba to pull him aside.

"Have you seen Clair?" he asked.

"No, I haven't been here long," Michael said. "But I think the cheerleaders are finished with their halftime routine."

"Good." Bubba gestured in the direction of Clark. "Who's that?"

"A friend of Alice's."

"Wonderful. He looks dead." Bubba turned to Kats, pulling out his wallet. "Get me a large buttered popcorn and a medium-size Dr Pepper without ice." He handed Kats a ten. "Treat yourself to whatever you want. Bring it to the fifty-yard line. But if I'm talking to Clair, keep your distance."

Kats accepted the money. The side of his face had begun to color from his bout with Nick. "Going to bag her, Bubba?"

"I'm going to wrap her up in aluminum foil and toast her. Go get in line. Tell them to watch the salt on the popcorn." When Kats was gone, Bubba said, "Let's do it, Mike."

"I'm waiting for Alice and Nick. I should stay here."

Bubba waved his hand. "Don't worry, they'll find you. Come on."

Michael really did want to see Bubba in action, especially going after Clair. He figured he'd be able to

70

catch Alice on her way back to Clark. And locating Nick would be no problem. He followed Bubba out onto the bleachers. The mood of the crowd appeared upbeat; Tabb High hadn't been down at halftime by only six points in years. The cheerleaders were gathered beneath the stands on the track, near center field. Standing nearest to the microphone, Clair was giving her voice a rest, sucking on a soft drink while waiting for the team to return to the field. With her shiny blond hair tied up in twin gold-ribboned ponytails, her legs deeply tanned beneath her short blue skirt, Michael had to admit she looked awfully sexy.

"Are you sure you want me with you?" Michael asked.

"I consider this a necessary part of your education. Just stay close, like we're hanging out together. But let me do all the talking."

A chest-high chain-link fence separated the audience from the track. Leaning casually into it, Bubba waved to Clair, calling, "Hey, come here. I want to talk to you."

Clair did not quite know what to make of the order. Holding on to her drink, she approached slowly. "Yeah, what?" she said, looking up at him.

Bubba smiled. "How are you doing, Clair? Good? You look good."

Clair took her straw out of her mouth. "I'm all right. What can I do for you, Bubba?"

Bubba rested an elbow on the top of the fence, dropped his smile for an unhappy expression. "I don't know, maybe you can do something. I'm having a bad day, a really bad time."

"What's wrong?" Clair asked.

"Well, like I was telling Mike here—you know Mike, sure you do—it's no wonder they speak of the stock market like it was a woman. You never know what she's going to do. The same day you think you've got her figured out, she turns around and stabs you in the back."

Clair showed interest. "Oh, yeah, someone told me you fooled around with stocks. What happened, did you lose some money?"

"It was all on paper, you understand. I was investing dollars I'd made on earlier trades. But it still pisses me off to be outguessed. I probably shouldn't talk about it. But the market, she's one nasty lady. How are things with you? I love your hair up like that. You should wear it like that all the time, even when you're taking a shower."

Clair played with one of her ponytails. "If I did that, I'd get my ribbons wet."

Michael recognized Bubba's strategy. It was Bubba's opinion that money and sex were inseparable in the female mind; thinking about credit cards and spending power, in his opinion, got them more excited than browsing through a *Playgirl* magazine.

"Then you could blow them dry," he said. "Hey, can I ask you something? This has really been a miserable day."

"What?"

"Let's go out together sometime. I'm always working, I've got to have more fun in life. Let's go out next weekend, next Saturday night."

Clair nodded. "Sure, we could—wait a second. I don't know. I don't think so. I'd like to, but I'm seeing Bill Skater. I don't think he'd like it if I went out with someone else."

Bubba waved his hand. Sometimes Michael thought Bubba could convince the pope to break his vows with a wave of that hand. "Bill won't, I know the guy. He doesn't want to totally monopolize your life. Don't worry about it, we'll have fun.'' He smiled. ''I just got new leather upholstery in my Jaguar.''

''That's right, you've got a Jag.''

''I sure do. Hey, you like music, Clair? You like U2?''

Bubba must have researched Clair's taste in music. She lit up. ''They're one of my favorite bands!''

''They're going to be in town next week. We'll go see them.''

''But I heard they were sold out.''

''I've already got tickets. Third row, dead center. We can eat first and then head on over to the Forum. Give me your phone number.''

Clair glanced around uneasily. Bubba had come a long way in less than a minute, but Clair was obviously hesitant about handing out her number to a short, overweight guy in front of the entire community. ''You really have third-row tickets?''

''They could be second row.''

She paused, sizing him up. She wasn't a total airhead. ''You're not just throwing me a line, are you? I've heard about you.''

Bubba was sly. ''What have you heard?''

Clair blushed. ''Stories.''

''Well, they're all true.'' Bubba leaned over the fence, spoke seriously. ''If you don't want to go, Clair, just say so. A lot of guys don't mind wasting their time. But I do.''

Michael had followed Bubba's moves perfectly up until this point. But when Clair suddenly blurted out her number, he realized he was completely lost.

''Five-five-five-four-three-two-six,'' she said. ''I don't have anything to write on. Will you remember it?''

Bubba nodded, moved back from the fence, straightening his jacket. ''I'll call you tomorrow.''

Clair returned to the microphone, her fellow cheerleaders quickly gathering around. Bubba led Michael back in the direction of the snack bar. "No sweat," he said.

Michael nodded. "All right, you were smooth. But if you hadn't brought up the concert, she would never have given you her number. Do you really have tickets in the third row?"

"Nope, I don't have any tickets. And I'm not going to pay scalper prices to get them."

"You're kidding? She'll freak when you pick her up."

"No, she won't. Ten minutes alone with me and she won't even remember how to spell U2."

Michael laughed. "I'd like to see that."

"I'm hoping you will. You noticed I made the date for next Saturday, and not tomorrow? I wanted to give you time to talk to Jessica Hart. We can make it a double date."

"I don't think I can move that fast."

"Then stop where you are and let her come to you." Bubba stopped, gestured toward midaisle. "She's coming down the steps now. See her? She's got that Sara chick with her."

Michael would not have believed his heart could start pounding so hard so quickly. Jessica had changed into white pants, a bright green blouse. A 35mm camera with a telephoto lens hung around her neck. Her long brown hair bounced with each step she took down the bleachers. He turned away.

"Let's get out of here," he said.

"Leave if you want. I've been looking forward to a private conversation with Jessie about her tastes in music."

"I'll stay," Michael grumbled. He hoped—and feared—that Jessica and Sara would pass them by without noticing them. Perhaps they would have. But Bubba stepped right into their path.

"Ladies," he said. "My name is Bubba. You may have heard of me. This is my friend, Michael. You may have heard of him, too. We are both fairly popular." He extended his hand. "We would like to welcome you to Tabb High."

Giggling, Jessica shook his hand, introducing herself. Sara was more reserved. "I *have* heard about you," she said. "This girl in my P.E. said I should watch out for you."

"Did she tell you why?" Bubba asked innocently.

"No."

"Then she must have a guilty conscience, and you shouldn't listen to her." Bubba pulled his gold pocket watch from his jacket. "I have a few minutes, Sara. Come with me. I want to discuss your political future."

"I'm not running for anything."

"But you like hot dogs, don't you?" Bubba asked.

Sara threw Jessica a quick glance. "I love hot dogs," she said slowly.

Bubba reached over and took Sara by the arm. "Then you should have one, with *everything* on it. Nice meeting you, Jessie. See you later, Mike."

When they were gone, Jessica continued to giggle. "Is he really your friend?" she asked.

"I think he considers me more of an apprentice." He cleared his throat. "I hope he doesn't overwhelm your friend."

"Sara can take care of herself."

"That's right, I almost forgot. I was there at lunch."

"I saw you when you sat down."

"Really?"

"Yeah."

The conversation ran into a hitch right there. Michael couldn't think of anything to say. Jessica started to fiddle with the focus on her camera. It was a Nikon 4004. The previous year, Michael had constructed an eight-inch reflector telescope. He had a dream of taking time-lapse photos of the sky through it from out in the desert. Jessica's camera would have been ideally suited for the job. Except it cost close to five hundred bucks.

"It's jammed again," she muttered, getting frustrated. A roar went up from the crowd. Wiping her hair out of her eyes, Jessica looked up. The team was coming back on the field. "Damn, the teacher wanted me to get a shot of the players running out of the tunnel."

"May I see it?" Michael asked.

"It does this all the time," she said, holding it out without removing the strap from her neck. He gently twisted the lens, trying not to brush up against her breasts; they weren't all that far away. She added, "I think I was sold an incompatible attachment."

It was indeed jammed. "Did you just take the telephoto lens out of its case and screw it in a moment ago?"

"Yeah, how did you know?"

"The camera's warm. You must have been holding it in your hands most of the night. But the lens is cool. Let them both sit out for a moment. When the temperatures average out, the jamming will stop."

She nodded. "That makes sense. You know a lot about cameras?"

He shrugged. "I've played around with a few."

"You should be the one taking these pictures, not me."

"Are you doing this for the paper or the yearbook?"

"Both, I guess." Jessica's attention wandered to the football players. She had a striking profile. He hadn't realized she had such thick lashes, such big eyes. He wondered what it would be like to touch her face.

"Who are you looking for?" he asked.

"A girlfriend."

"Is she on the football team?"

"She plays quarterback." Jessica turned his way again. "Hey, do you know a guy named Russ Desmond?"

Michael felt a pang of jealousy. "Yeah. But he's not on the football team this year."

"He runs cross-country, right?"

"Yeah."

"Do you know him well?"

"Not really."

Jessica smiled. "I suppose I can trust you. Sara's been searching for him all night."

Michael felt better. "She's searching in the wrong place. Russ would never come to a football game."

"Why not?"

"He hates the coach. And the coach hates him. It's a long story."

Jessica nodded, her lovely brown eyes drifting up into the stands this time. "Where is she?" she whispered.

"Sara?"

"No, the girlfriend I mentioned. You wouldn't know her. She's from Mesa. She's only a sophomore, an old friend." Jessica chuckled. "All day she's been telling me about this fantastic guy I've got to meet."

"What's her name?"

"Alice McCoy."

Michael leaned into the fence. He was lucky he didn't flip over and land on the track. "Oh, my," he said.

"Pardon?"

"Nothing."

Jessica suddenly turned her head toward the field. Tall, blond, and handsome number sixteen was walking toward the sidelines. Jessica quickly raised her camera, trying to focus her jammed telephoto lens. "Damn," she muttered.

Had Jessica not tried so eagerly to take Bill Skater's picture at that precise moment, Michael probably would have admitted he was the fantastic guy Alice wanted Jessica to meet. Later, he was to wonder if he *had* told Jessica, if the tragedy that was to follow Alice's party would have been avoided. It would be a possibility that would haunt him the entire year. It would be a possibility based solely upon a young girl's strange dream.

"You might want to give it a few more minutes," he said softly.

Jessica did not appear to hear him. She had lowered the camera, and her eyes. Bill had stopped at the microphone to talk to Clair.

"I better go," Michael said.

Jessica raised her head. "Huh? No, don't go, please. I'm sorry. What were you saying?"

"Nothing." He edged away. "I really have to go."

"That's too bad. Thanks!"

"For what?"

She forced a smile. "For everything, what else?"

Michael did not head in the direction of the snack bar, but away from it. Alice would have to forgive him for ditching her. He couldn't bear the thought of witnessing Jessica's probable—if she went for the likes of Bill Skater, it was virtually certain—disappointment when she learned Michael Olson was Mr. Fantastic.

He only remembered that Nick had gone for their dinner when Nick came up to him with a box full of goodies.

"I hope you like junk food," Nick said. "I live on it."

Michael accepted a hot dog, a tub of popcorn, and a large orange. Nick again refused Michael's offer to help pay for the stuff. They continued to walk in the direction of the scoreboard. "I bet you've had to search all over for me," Michael said. "Sorry I took off."

"I knew where you were," Nick said. "I was watching you talk to that girl."

"Jessica? You should have come over. I could have introduced you."

"No, I couldn't do that."

"Why not?"

"I don't know. I would have gotten in your way."

"Don't say that."

Nick glanced over at him. For an instant, something glimmered deep within Nick's black eyes. But all he said was "OK, Mike."

They sat at the end of the bleachers, away from the crowd. Nick began to dig into his food. Michael realized he'd lost his appetite. He sipped his drink, stared at the clock on the scoreboard. He didn't even know what he was doing at the game. She had smiled at him, thanked him, all the while thinking about the quarterback. Bubba would steal Clair away from Bill. Bill would find solace in Jessica's arms.

It's like the earth going around the sun—a vicious cycle.

"This is going to be a long second half," he muttered, referring to the rest of his life.

"Want to leave?"

"Do you?"

"Whatever you want, Mike."

"Whatever I want," he repeated quietly. He chuckled sadly, shook his head. "No, not today. Maybe

79

tomorrow." He slapped Nick on the back. At least he'd made a new friend. "Tell me about yourself, Nick?"

"What do you want to hear?"

"Everything." He thought of Jessica's line. "What else?"

It took them awhile until they returned to the topic of girls. Finally, however, Michael heard of Maria, and spoke of Jessica. They both agreed that something had to change.

CHAPTER
SIX

Polly McCoy noticed that her arm was bleeding. A drop of red trailed from beneath the bandage inside her left elbow all the way to her wrist. She had given blood that afternoon; it was a habit of hers to give blood every two months, as frequently as she could. Once Jessica had joked that she must have been a vampire in a past life, that she was working off karma. Polly didn't know about that. She had all this money and she had never done anything to earn it. She felt as if she had to help people, give something back. And she didn't believe in reincarnation, anyway, or even life after death. When you died, you were dead. It was pretty simple. On the other hand, she occasionally did wonder about vampires, about demons in general. So many terrible things happened to so many nice people. There had to be something evil behind it all.

Taking out a Kleenex and wiping away the blood, Polly saw Alice making her way up the stadium steps. Polly was sitting in the very top row. She liked the view. She could see what everyone was up to. Of course, when halftime finished, she would rejoin Sara and Jessica closer to the field. They had all come together. But for now she didn't mind being alone. Actually, she preferred it. She was not in the best of moods. She was mad at her sister. Sara and Jessica had been looking for him, but only she had seen Clark. She'd watched him and Alice carrying on the whole night.

And it was me who saw him first.

Polly had met Clark three months ago, during the last week of school at Mesa High. The day had been beautiful. She and Alice had decided to go for a hike in the woods. They had driven up into the nearby mountains and set out along a trail adjacent to a stream. They quickly ran into trouble.

Approximately two miles from the car, Polly stepped on a loose stone and twisted her ankle. The sprain was nasty. They both decided she should stay where she was while Alice went for help. While waiting for her sister's return, Clark appeared.

Polly's initial reaction to him had been one of fear. He talked weird. He looked weirder. But he had a certain *touch*. When he took her swollen ankle in his delicate hands—over her shy protests—and began to massage points on either side of the bone, the pain vanished. Polly had read about acupressure and stuff like that. What he did went beyond that. The swelling even stopped.

And the more she listened to his voice, the less strange it sounded. He had lots of interesting ideas. He told her how the mountain they were on had once been used by the Indians as a sacred spot for the channeling of the spirits of long-dead medicine men. What made his point of view so unique was that he neither believed nor disbelieved what he said. He was just being "open." He told her she had to open up. He had a pad and pencil with him. He wanted her to take off her top and let him sketch her. When she refused, he began to draw her as if she were completely nude. He finished the sketch minutes before Alice returned with the ranger. He gave it to her as a present. She didn't remember having given him her number. But he called her the next day.

Over the next two months, they never went out once. They spent most of their time together necking in her bedroom with the door locked. She finally did take her top off for him, and her pants, but they never had sex. He would push her right to the limit and then back off. She knew it was probably for the best—what with all the talk of herpes and AIDS going around—nevertheless, it still frustrated her. She wondered if he truly found her attractive. She wondered that a lot when he started chasing Alice.

It happened just like that. Overnight. Hello, how are you, Polly? Let me speak to Alice. And from then on Alice and Clark were always together. The only thing that kept Polly from freaking out all together was that their relationship appeared to be a brother-sister sort of thing. Alice said it was, and of course being the considerate sister that she was, she had still asked Polly a thousand times if it was OK. Polly told her not to worry. She wanted what was best for Alice. And there was no denying Clark was "opening" her up to all kinds of artistic inspirations. Alice had paintings in progress in her studio that the special-effects people in Hollywood couldn't have dreamed of.

Yet Polly was finally beginning to wonder if she hadn't gotten a raw deal. Tonight, for the first time, she had seen Clark put his arm around Alice. If you would do that in public, there were a lot of other things you might do in private. Clark had such hypnotic green eyes, like a cat. And those long fingers. She couldn't stand the thought of them all over her baby sister.

"Hi. Have you see Jessie?" Alice asked, panting from her hop up the steps.

"Last time I saw her, she was down by the cheer-leaders. But she's not there now."

Alice searched the stands, sighing. "I've got to find her right away. Clark wants to leave."

"I could give her a message for you."

"No, it's not that. I want her to meet somebody."

"Why are you leaving with Clark now?"

"I told you, he wants to leave."

"Why does he want to leave?"

"He didn't tell me." Alice stopped. "What's wrong?"

"With my arm? It's bleeding, can't you see? I gave blood today. You should, too, sometime. There're a lot of sick people out there who need it."

"No, I mean, you sound mad?"

"Why would I be mad?"

"I don't know."

"I'm not mad."

Alice smiled. Polly could remember the first time Alice had ever smiled. Polly had only been two years old at the time, and Alice two months, but Polly remembered everything. "Are you having fun?" Alice asked.

"Sure. How about you?"

Alice beamed at the whole stadium. "I'm having a great time. I love this school. I love the people here." Suddenly she leaned over and embraced her sister. "And I love you most of all!"

Polly returned the hug. "I know you do," she said softly, feeling the bones of Alice's rib cage under her fingers. When they had both been kids, Alice had tended toward chubbiness. Now, Polly could barely get her to eat one full meal a day. "Would you like a candy bar?" she asked, reaching for her purse.

Alice straightened herself. "No, chocolate gives me acne."

"It doesn't do that to me," Polly replied, getting the candy out for herself. The nurse at the hospital this afternoon had told her to go home and have a big meal. She had to make up for what she had lost. She didn't appreciate Alice suddenly staring at her as if she were a pig. "I gave blood today," she repeated.

"What about your diet?"

"Leave me alone, all right?"

Alice knelt back down beside her, holding her hands. "Are you upset 'cause Clark's here?"

Polly swallowed on the lump in her throat. "No. I see Clark all the time at the house. What difference should it make seeing him here? Anyway, why have you been hiding him away all night? Jessie and Sara want to meet him."

Alice leaned back on her heels. "I don't want them to see him."

"Then why did you bring him here tonight?"

A note of anger entered her voice. "I didn't. He insisted he come. Now he wants to leave early." She looked away, her expression strangely flat. "I've got to get away from him," she whispered.

Polly felt a thrill. She softened her voice. "Why?"

"He's not very nice."

"What?"

"He talks about mom and dad."

Polly closed her eyes, the thrill gone. "What does he say?"

"Nothing."

"Tell me!"

"No, it has nothing to do with you."

Polly opened her eyes, took a bite of her candy, smiled slowly. "All right, let's drop it. Let's talk about the party."

Alice brightened. "Can we have it?"

Polly nodded. The bad moment had come, and the bad moment had gone. All of a sudden she felt greatly relieved. "Yes, I think it would be all right. But we'll have to take Aunty over to Uncle Tom's for the night. The noise might upset her."

Alice nodded, leaned over, and kissed her cheek. "Thanks! I owe you a million."

Polly smiled at her. "You only owe me a penny. Don't invite Clark to the party."

Alice didn't hesitate. "I won't even tell him we're having one."

Alice left to search for Jessica. Polly remembered a textbook she had forgotten to take home that afternoon. She debated about waiting until after the game to get it from her locker. She finally decided that Sara would get mad if she did. Sara had been getting mad at her a lot lately; it was really beginning to bother her.

Polly accidentally ran into Sara at the bottom of the steps.

"Do you know where Jessie is?" Sara demanded.

"No. Alice doesn't either."

"What are you talking about? Where is Alice?"

"I don't know."

Sara rubbed her stomach, groaned. "I just ate three hot dogs."

"Why three?"

"My political adviser insisted. Where are you going?"

"To my locker."

"Is the locker hallway open now?"

"The door lock is busted. It's always open."

"What did you forget?"

"Nothing. Don't say anything mean."

Sara laughed loudly. "Don't get mugged. I could

see the school from the snack bar. They don't waste electricity here. There isn't a light on.''

No greater truth had ever passed Sara's lips. After leaving the stadium and heading around the silent gymnasium, Polly found herself in a disquieting land of darkness. Tabb High had a lot of trees. The branches blocked much of the sky, as did the overhanging roofs. She wished she had a flashlight. She had never cared much for the dark. It had been on a dark and lonely road her parents had died. She remembered it well. She remembered everything.

What did that bastard say about them?

Her steps echoed softly as she strode down the empty open hallway. She was uneasy, yes, but she also enjoyed the emptiness. Sometimes during the day she wished she could be this alone, strolling the campus free and easy, meeting only those people she chose to meet, hearing only those voices she wanted to hear, touching only those who wanted to touch her. . . .

What did Clark say about me?

Polly was crossing the courtyard, passing beneath what she had heard referred to as the varsity tree, when the can landed on top of her head. It startled her something awful; she practically had a heart attack right there on the spot. She jumped away from the tree and cried in a trembling voice, "Who's there!?''

A vague figure shifted above her in the branches. She leaned slightly forward—all the while telling herself to run the other way—straining to see better. "Hello?'' she croaked.

The figure croaked back. No, it was more of a belch. She reached down, picked up the can that had struck her on the head, smelled the beer. Her fear disappeared as quickly as it had come. Somebody was just getting drunk in private. Laughing, she walked toward the tree trunk.

"Hey, if I was you, I wouldn't be drinking up there. You could slip and hurt—"

A flash of metal and wood whipped by, inches from her face. Polly leapt back a step. Embedded in the ground in the grass at her feet was a huge axe.

Polly screamed bloody murder.

The guy fell out of the tree. Polly kept screaming. He rolled over and looked up at her. "What time is it?" he mumbled.

Polly bit her lip. "Past nine-thirty."

The guy sat up, rubbed his head. "Where are the birds?"

"What birds?"

"I heard birds." He burped again, deep and loud, and reached for his axe.

"That was me. Excuse me, what are you doing with that?"

He was using it, Polly realized a moment later, to climb to his feet. She relaxed a notch. There were empty beer cans littering the ground. This guy wouldn't be chasing her anywhere.

"Do you need some help?" she asked tentatively. He briefly gained an upright position, clinging to the axe handle, before swaying forward and smacking his skull directly into the tree trunk. "Oh, no!" she cried, jumping to his side. "You'll kill yourself."

"What time is it?" he breathed in her face. With the lack of light, she couldn't see what he looked like. She could, however, smell him. He must have poured half the beer over his shirt.

"I told you, past nine-thirty. Why do you keep asking me that?"

He tried to get up again. "Got to chop this down before morning, before the birds get here."

"You can't do that." She tried to pull the axe from his hands. "No."

He wouldn't let go of the handle. "Why not?"

"Because it's a pretty tree. Leave it alone."

The guy turned, stared at the trunk, and then spat on it. "Those faggot foots—footballs. They all stand here." He leaned into the axe, pushed himself up. "It's got to go."

Polly moved back a step. He'd raised the axe over his head. It looked capable of flying in a dozen different directions. "Stop!" she pleaded.

He let go with a wild swing. The tip of the axe sliced into the bark. Leaning back, he tried to pull it free. His hands ended up slipping from the handle, and he was back on his ass. Before he could get up, Polly knelt by his side, putting both her palms on his chest. Even through his soggy shirt, she could feel the curves of his well-developed pectoral muscles. "Look, you've got to stop. If you kill this tree, you'll be killing all the birds who live in it."

"I can't hurt the birds," he said, trying repeatedly to get up, not realizing it was she that was holding him down.

"That's right. So why don't we take your nice axe and put it in my car and I'll drive you home." She wasn't exactly sure why she had made the offer. It could have been because of some distant streetlight. A sliver of white had fallen across his face, revealing a rugged—rough would probably have been closer to the truth—handsomeness. He belched again, his jaw dropping open.

"Is it you?" he asked, amazed.

"Who? What?"

"You! I stopped the race for you. The foots—Coach made them kick me off the team. All because of you."

"No, it wasn't me."

He wiped the back of his arm across his nose. "You're pretty, Sara."

"Thank you. Let me take you home."

"Your place or mine?" he slurred as she helped him up.

"Your place. What's your name?"

"Rusty—Russ."

"I'm Polly."

"Sara Polly?"

"I'm whoever you want me to be."

It took time getting the axe out of the tree. It took longer getting Russ and the axe into her car. Fortunately, he remembered where he lived. She assumed it was the right house. She deposited him in the front yard without knocking on the front door and then headed back for the stadium. She decided to keep the axe for now. In his intoxicated condition, there was no telling what he might do with it.

She liked him. And she didn't care that he was the guy Sara had been searching for all night. She'd seen Clark first and look where that had gotten her. Nowhere.

When it came to love, you were a fool to be nice.

CHAPTER SEVEN

Mr. Bark stopped Sara the following Monday morning as she was leaving his political science class. Jessica was with her.

"What is it?" Sara asked defensively. "I stayed awake the whole period."

"It's not that. I have some news for you." He paused, and there was no denying from his expression that he thought it was bad news. "You know I am the faculty adviser to the student government?"

"It doesn't surprise me," Sara said cautiously. "What's up?"

"You've been elected student body president."

Sara laughed. "What the hell? No, you're kidding. What are you talking about?"

"You were elected by a landslide."

Sara swallowed. "But I wasn't running. Jessie, tell him it was all a joke."

"You didn't want to be president?" Jessica asked in surprise.

"Your name was on the ballot," Mr. Bark said.

"Now hold on a second," Sara said. "I explained

this to the whole school last Friday. Jessie put my name down."

Jessica smiled. This was great. "No, I didn't."

"Polly did then. It makes no difference. I can't be president. I hate politics. I hate politicians. No, absolutely not."

"I don't want you as president, either," Mr. Bark said. "I think you have a bad attitude. But the student body doesn't think so. Your nearest competitor didn't get a quarter of your votes. You have a responsibility to your peers. There's a lot of business that has to be taken care of immediately. We don't have time for another election."

"Who's the new vice-president?" Sara asked.

"Clair Hilrey."

"I thought she was running for president," Jessica said.

Mr. Bark frowned. "I thought she was, too. Maybe she put herself down for both offices. She shouldn't have done that."

"Make her president," Sara said quickly.

"I can't do that," Mr. Bark said.

"Then I'll do it," Sara said.

"No, you can't do that, either. It's against the rules."

"The President of the country never follows the rules, why should I? No, wait. If you won't accept my resignation this instant, I'll intentionally break every rule in the book. Then you'll have to impeach me."

Mr. Bark was getting angry. "You don't impeach student body presidents."

"Why not? This is a free and vicious society."

"Why are you being so difficult? There are kids in this school who would give almost anything to have the honor that's been bestowed on you."

Sara started to speak, stopped, silently shook her head.

"It might be fun," Jessica said. "It might make you popular."

Sara glared at her. "No," she said firmly.

Mr. Bark had run out of patience. "I can't stand here all day arguing with you. We're having our first student council meeting tomorrow at lunch in Room H-Sixteen. If you should change your mind and want to accept the office, see me sometime this afternoon. There're notes on the student body's financial status you should go through before the meeting. If not, then I guess we'll have to carry on without you."

Jessica had chemistry next. She had to go. Once outside Mr. Bark's class, Sara refused to speak to her, anyway. She went off in a huff. Jessica couldn't help laughing.

The laughter did not stay with her. She'd had a miserable weekend. She was still sleepy and tired from her travels. She'd had to take long naps Saturday and Sunday afternoons just to be awake at dinnertime. Also, she'd been lamenting Bill Skater's obvious interest in Clair Hilrey. The disappointment was silly, she knew. She had only started at the school. She couldn't realistically expect the resident fox not to have some sort of girlfriend. Nevertheless, she had spent hours since the football game wondering how she could get his attention. In Mr. Bark's class just now, Bill hadn't looked at her once. And she'd worn her shortest skirt.

Her gloom deepened when her chemistry teacher announced a surprise quiz in the middle of lab. She practically fell off her stool. "He didn't say anything about a quiz on Friday," she complained to her lab partner, Maria.

"Last Monday he warned us to be ready for a quiz at any time," Maria said, pushing aside their rows of test tubes, getting out a fresh sheet of paper. "You weren't here. But I wouldn't worry, it shouldn't count for much."

Jessica worried anyway. To get accepted at Stanford, she had to keep her GPA close to a perfect four. She hadn't even glanced at the textbook over the weekend.

The teacher let them stay at their lab desks. He wrote several molecular formulas on the board and asked for their valence values. It appeared no big deal for the bulk of the class; they went right to it. Jessica sat staring at the board. She'd left her glasses at home again. She could hardly read the formulas.

What's a valence value?

When Jessica finally looked down, she saw that Maria had slipped her a piece of paper with two rows of positive and negative values. Sitting across the gray-topped table, Maria nodded.

"I can't," Jessica whispered.

"Just this once," Maria whispered back.

The teacher wasn't watching. Jessica scribbled the numbers onto her paper. The teacher collected them a few minutes later. Then he wrote the answers on the board. Maria knew her stuff; they each got a hundred. Jessica thanked her as they returned to the lab.

"I've never cheated before," she said, embarrassed.

"But you didn't know there could be a quiz," Maria said, adding softly, "Sometimes it's hard not to lie."

"Well, if I can ever make it up to you, let me know."

Maria nodded—she didn't talk a lot—and they continued with their acid-base reactions, which made no more sense than they had before the quiz. Jessica swore to herself that she would study chemistry for at least two hours every night until she caught up. She even entertained the idea of asking Michael Olson for a couple of tutorial lessons. She wasn't getting much out of the teacher; he talked too fast, and seemingly in a foreign language. Michael obviously had a sharp mind. She'd felt rather silly when she'd needed his help at the game with the camera. He had been right about the jamming disappearing when the temperatures evened out. Although she found his intelligence somewhat intimidating, he was easy to talk to. Yet she worried what he thought of her. He would start out friendly enough, and then after a couple of minutes talking to her, he'd be in a hurry to get away.

He probably thinks I'm an airhead.

Sara had cooled off by lunch. When Jessica met her near the snack bar, she even laughed about how her election had proved beyond doubt the substandard intelligence of the majority of Tabb's students. She had not changed her mind about the job.

Polly joined them midway through break. She had not heard of the election results, and neither Jessica nor Sara brought it up. She had, however, already printed up the party invitations—elegantly lettered orange cards in flowery orange envelopes. Jessica and Sara both agreed the printers had done a fine job. Polly gave them six each.

"But don't invite anyone weird," she warned.

"You'll have to give one to Russ," Jessica told Sara.

She fingered the envelopes uneasily. "I'll think about it."

"Are you talking about Russ Desmond?" Polly asked suddenly.

"Yes," Sara said warily.

Polly giggled. "You can't invite him. You're the one who got him kicked off the cross-country team. He hates you."

Sara didn't respond immediately, which surprised Jessica. "What are you talking about?" Jessica asked.

"Russ had to stop in the middle of his race last

95

Friday to help Sara up. She had jumped right in his way, and he accidentally knocked her down. He ended up losing the race, and the football coach got furious and kicked him off the team."

"How does the football coach have the authority to kick someone off the cross-country team?" Jessica asked. Sara had told her about the race incident, but from a slightly different perspective.

"He's also the athletic director," Polly said.

An odd look had crossed Sara's face. She was angry, certainly, but also—was it possible?—upset. "You lie," she said.

"I'm not," Polly said indignantly. "The whole school knows about it."

"If that's true, then why did the whole school just nominate me president?"

Polly sneered. "Since when are you president?"

"I am president. Ain't I president, Jessie?"

"Unquestionably. But why does Russ hate Sara? He can't blame her for what happened."

Polly shrugged. "He does."

"How do *you* know?" Sara demanded.

"He told me so when I took him home Friday night."

Sara snorted. "You took him home? Where did you take him home from?"

"It's none of your business," Polly said.

Sara held up her finger. "Polly, if you're lying to me, or even if you're telling me the truth, you're going to have a party at your house you're never going to forget 'cause I'm going to drown you in your goddamn swimming pool."

And with that, Sara whirled around and stalked off.

"What's gotten into her?" Polly asked.

"I don't know," Jessica said. "Maybe it's love."

Polly departed to eat large quantities of sugar. Jessica was left holding her six invitations and wondering who to give them to. It took her all of a fraction of a second to realize she had to get one to Bill Skater. It didn't take her much longer to spot him. He was alone, walking toward the parking lot. She had never seen him alone before; he usually had a bunch of guys around him. This could be a rare opportunity. Quickly she strode toward the other exit. She should be able to circle around a portion of the lot and run into him coming the other way.

Her plan worked better than she expected. She ended up coming up the aisle where he'd parked his car. He stopped when he saw her, nodded.

"Hi."

She looked up, smiled. "Hi! You look familiar. Do we share a class?"

He put the key to his red Corvette in the door, his eyes on her. They were as blue as the Bill in her fantasies. "I don't think so," he said. "What's your name?"

"Mr. Bark. I mean, we're in Mr. Bark's class together. My name's Jessie. What's yours, Bill? Is your name Bill?"

He nodded. He did not appear to notice she was suffering from momentary brain damage. She was so nervous. "I remember you," he said. "You sit next to the girl who snores."

What notoriety. "That's me," she gushed.

"Right." He opened his car door. "See you around, Joan."

"Jessie. Wait!"

He sat inside on the black leather upholstery. "Yes?"

"Ah—you were great last Friday, you know, in the game. I thought you were." Tabb had lost sixteen to three. Bill had thrown only one interception and an equal number of completions.

"Thanks. Bye."

"Bye. Would you like to go to a party?"

He shut his car door, rolled down his window. "What did you say?"

"My friend's having a party. She gave me all these to pass out." Jessica waved her half-dozen invitations as if they might multiply into hundreds any second. "Would you like come? It's not this Saturday, but next Saturday. In the evening."

He took one of the envelopes, opened it, nodding as he read the contents. "Are you going to be there?" he asked.

"Sure, yeah. The whole time."

He nodded again, tossing the card onto the passenger seat. "I'll see you then."

He drove away. Her approach had set women's lib back twenty years, she realized. But she didn't care! He had asked if she'd be there! He was only coming to see her!

Right, and your name's Joan.

Jessica decided to dwell on the positive. It didn't require much willpower. She floated back up the steps and into the courtyard. She bought a milk and sat by herself in the shade beneath a tree. Polly had specified on the cards that everyone was to bring a bathing suit. Jessica had a new bikini she could wear—blue with white polka dots. It left little to the imagination. Maybe he would bump up against her in the water . . .

If she went in the water. She'd almost drowned as a child in a backyard pool. She didn't know how to swim.

Jessica looked up. Michael Olson was coming over to say hi. How sweet.

*　　*　　*

They were in the computer room. Nick was listening. Bubba was talking. Michael wanted to get it over with. They had finally decided to do it, Nick and himself. They were going to ask the girls out.

"It's important you do everything in its proper order," Bubba was saying. "Get her alone. Start a conversation. Bring up a movie. A movie doesn't sound as heavy as dinner. Of course, once you're on the date, you can always go to dinner. But it's easy to work a movie into the conversation. Do each of you know what's playing?"

"Yes," Michael said.

"No," Nick said, hanging on to Bubba's every word. He had looked more relaxed during Kats's holdup. Then again, Michael wasn't exactly enjoying a period of low blood pressure. It struck him as ironic that the fear of one little word could have such an effect on two grown boys. Would you like to get together this weekend?

No.

A big little word.

"It doesn't matter," Bubba continued. "She'll know what's playing. Then ask if she's busy this weekend. This is a better question than asking outright if she'd like to go out. It eliminates a possible objection before she can raise it."

"But you asked Clair outright?" Michael said.

"Yes, but neither of you is Bubba. Now, after she has said no—"

"What if she is busy?" Nick interrupted.

"Then ask about another time. Don't be discouraged if this weekend is not good. Even teenage girls have other commitments. But if she puts you off twice, then back off. Keep your dignity."

"Go on," Nick said.

"Arrange the date. Set a definite time and get her phone number and address. Be sure to paint a picture that the whole thing is casual. That way she'll know how to dress without asking. Also, you don't want her to think she's overly important to you."

"Get off it," Michael said.

Bubba spoke seriously. "That may offend your romantic ideals, Mike, but it's a fact the human animal only desires what it can't have. True, you have to make her feel wanted, but never *loved*. If she knows you can't live without her, then she'll also know she can see you whenever she wants. You want to operate from a position of strength. Always keep her in the dark, unsure of where she stands."

"Go on," Nick said again.

"That's it, for now. When the date's set, come back here and I'll give you the next lesson: how to get her clothes off."

"We have a problem," Michael said. "Nick doesn't have a car."

"Let him borrow yours," Bubba said.

"Then what is Mike supposed to use?" Nick asked.

"He can borrow my car. And I'll get Clair to pick me up."

"You'll make her drive, and you don't even have the concert tickets?" Michael asked.

Bubba smiled. "Mike, you worry about the most unimportant things." He stood and slapped them both on the back. "Make me proud of you, boys."

Michael and Nick left Bubba to his computers. Lunch was more than half over. They had to locate the girls quickly. They hurried toward the courtyard.

"Why are we doing this?" Michael muttered.

"We don't have to," Nick said with more than a note of hope in his voice.

"Let's not start that again." They had talked about

this moment all weekend at work. Without this mutual encouragement, Michael realized, neither of them would have gotten this far. Yet Michael had another reason for having decided to ask Jessica out. He'd had a dream.

It had been beautiful. He had been on a roped bridge stretching between two lands, one a desolate desert, the other a lush green forest. There had been a churning river running beneath his feet, and above—in contrast to the brightly lit lands—a black sky adorned with countless stars. He had been standing in the middle of the bridge facing the desert, hesitating, when a female voice had spoken at his back.

"I will follow you," she said. And when he started to turn around, she added quickly, "No, don't. You can't see me."

"Why not?"

"Because of the veil. I'm still wearing it. But you're young. Go forward, I will follow you."

The desert beyond looked most unappealing, particularly compared to the green woods that he could glimpse out the corner of his eye. "Who are you?" he asked.

"You have forgotten." There was no censure in her voice, only mild amusement and a rich, enduring love. Michael could almost, but not quite, figure out who it was. "It happens sometimes. It doesn't matter. Just remember that I am behind you. That you can't fall. No, don't look down, either. Go forward."

"Then can I see you?"

"Yes, but not today. Later, another time. I will see you first, and then we will meet again, like we always do. Go now, and don't be afraid. You are my love, Michael Olson. . . ."

And then he had woken up, and the stars outside were fading with the approaching dawn. He hadn't gone back to sleep. He had just lain there feeling content. That had been Saturday morning.

The dream had left him with a measure of courage. Enough to risk the big No. Walking beside Nick, he continued to wonder who the girl had been.

They split up when they reached the center of campus. Nick had spotted Maria. She was by herself, next to the low adobe wall that surrounded Tabb. Michael wished him luck. He had to chuckle when Nick crossed himself.

Michael sighted Jessica minutes later. She was sitting alone beneath a tree, drinking a milk. And he had thought Nick superstitious; he would have recited a Hail Mary on the spot had he been able to remember the opening line. Jessica waved to him. He was trapped.

"How are you doing?" she asked as he approached. She looked positively radiant. Could she be this happy to see him?

"Fine. How about you?"

"Fantastic." She patted the grass beside her. "Have a seat. I was just thinking about you today, in chemistry class."

He sat down. The ground felt solid, better than his feet. "Really? I thought they only studied guys like me in psychology."

She laughed, and he secretly congratulated himself on his witty remark. "No, I was remembering how you wrote the lab manual they use."

Michael almost gagged. "Who told you that?"

She paused. "It's not true?"

"No. All I did last year was discover a couple of procedural errors in the manual. I didn't write it." He smiled. "I am still in high school, after all."

She laughed. "With your reputation, it's hard to remember that."

Michael had never thought of himself as having a reputation. "Are you having trouble in the class?" he asked.

She set down her milk, folded her hands between her bare legs. He couldn't help noticing how much of her legs there was to notice. Nice skirt. Nice legs. "Yes," she admitted quietly. "I think missing the first week has thrown me off. We had a quiz today, and I didn't even know what the questions meant."

"Did you flunk it?"

She giggled. "No, I got an A." She continued in a serious voice, "No, I really am confused. And I was wondering if maybe you could possibly tutor me a tiny bit? I could pay you for your time and all." She looked at him with her big brown eyes. "I really need the grade, Michael. My parents are on top of me all the time about my GPA."

He couldn't believe his luck. It almost seemed unnatural. A corner of his mind wondered if Bubba had not somehow set it up. "Sure, I could help you. But you wouldn't have to pay me. I think you'll catch on quickly, once you get used to the chemical language. Physics, calculus, chemistry—they all have a jargon that can be frightening at first. I sometimes think scientists keep it that way to make themselves look smart. Honestly, chemistry is as easy as basic math."

"I have a lot of trouble with that, too."

"When do you want to start?"

"I want to do something for you first." She brightened. "I know what! I'll take you to a movie. Yeah, that would be fair. I pay for the movie and you teach me about valence values. How does that sound?"

Michael had to take a breath. Very unnatural, this whole conversation. "I have some free time this Saturday. Can you get by in class until then?"

"Yeah, we won't have another quiz that soon." She pulled a pen from her purse, began to write on one of the funny orange envelopes by her side. "I'll give you my number and address, and you give me yours. If you want, I can drive."

"No, that's OK, I have a car." He would have a Jaguar Saturday night. He began to feel rather happy about the whole dating business. All these lonely years he had suffered in silence. There was nothing to it. All you had to do was decide to ask them out and then they asked you. Sure.

This won't happen again in another three hundred years.

They exchanged the vital information. He noticed she lived in Lemon Grove. Big bucks. Maybe he wouldn't tell her he had borrowed the Jag. He nodded to the orange envelope in his hand. "What is this?"

"Oh, an invitation to a party my friend's having. Alice McCoy—I told you about her at the game? You're welcome to come."

His heart skipped as it had last Friday when she had mentioned Alice's name. But this time the reasons were different. This time there was no reason at all, only the voice in the dream. *"I will follow you."* Why would Alice have been standing behind him, covered in a veil? Even his subconscious should have a purpose in putting her there.

"Thanks." He began to get up. He didn't think he would go to the party. He would have to be Mr. Fantastic again. For now, he was doing all right as Michael Olson. He hadn't seen Alice at school today. He hoped she wasn't sick. "I've got to go," he said.

Jessica looked up, surprised, got slowly to her feet, brushing off her bottom. "I didn't mean to keep you."

"You haven't. I'm not that busy. I'll give you a call."

She smiled. "Or leave me a note in our locker. I seem to keep missing you between classes."

He had missed her on purpose today. "We'll talk," he said, turning away. "Take it easy."

"Bye!"

He wanted to be happy. He had been looking forward to this moment—he had better be happy. He was going out with Jessica Hart, he told himself. She was sweet, beautiful, charming. He had her number. She needed him. Bubba would be proud of him. . . .

Do you want her to need you? Or to care about you?

He decided, as long as he got to see her, *he* didn't care.

He hoped Nick was all right.

"Hello, Nick," Maria said. "How's your head?"

"My head? It's OK."

She put down her sack. It appeared packed with oranges, nothing else. He felt as if he had an orange stuck between his ears. He couldn't remember what Bubba had told him to say first. "The swelling looks like it's gone down?"

"Yeah."

She nodded. "Would you like an orange?"

Nick accepted the fruit. "You have a lot of them."

"My dad brings them home."

Her dad probably worked the orchards. The possibility reinforced his suspicion she had not been in the country more than a year, two at the outside, that her father was working for slave wages picking the fruit. Bubba had told him to bring up the movies. "You can't get oranges like these at the movies."

Maria blinked. "They don't sell them there."

"Yeah, that's what I mean." He put his hand on the nearby wall for support. Unfortunately, he used the hand that held the orange, and crushed it. A squirt of juice hit Maria right in the eyes. "Damnit, I'm sorry!" he cried, dropping the offending fruit. She calmly reached for a handkerchief in her bag.

"You got a ripe one," she said.

"I'm really sorry."

"It's nothing."

"It must hurt."

She looked up at him, her face serious. "If I ever did get hurt, I don't think I could take it like you did last Friday."

"That was nothing."

"Someone told me this morning that you got thrown into a mirror."

Nick scratched his head. "Well, yeah, I didn't walk into it." She liked that. She smiled. She was the kind of girl who needed to smile more often. So solemn.

"Would you like another orange?" she asked.

He waved it away, feeling a sudden surge of confidence. She admired how he had fought! She wasn't afraid of him. "Would you like to go to the movies Saturday night?"

She nodded. "Could you pick me up at the library? I'll be there studying."

"I could, yeah." He would have to ask Michael where the library was. "What time would be good?"

"Six. That's when the library closes."

That Bubba was a genius. "I'll see you then."

CHAPTER
EIGHT

Sara had decided to attend the student council meeting Tuesday at lunch after all. When she arrived with Mr. Bark's papers on the financial status of the council tucked under her arm, the other officers were already gathered around the large table in Room H-16. She recognized only three: Clair Hilrey, Bill Skater, and that football player everyone called The Rock. She knew of the latter because of the stories that had been circulating about his fight with the tall black guy. The Rock sat slightly hunched over in his chair. He had not played in Friday's game. Sara heard the black guy had almost killed him.

Two adults were also present: Mr. Bark and Tabb's principal, Mr. Smith, both sitting unobtrusively in one corner. They were there to oversee, she had heard, not to interfere. The promise of the principal's presence was one of the reasons she had decided to come. She hoped to speak to him about allowing Russ Desmond back on the cross-country team. That lying Polly had been feeding her a line—there was no doubt about that—but she did feel somewhat guilty about having stepped in his way. She certainly didn't want him hating her.

Another factor had brought her to the meeting. The biggest problem she had with school, and life in general, was that it bored her. After thinking about it awhile, she had come to the conclusion that being president couldn't make the situation any worse. Of course, if the job ever got to be more of a hassle than it was worth, she could always walk away from it—and to hell with any responsibility she owed to her peers.

"Have you been waiting for me?" Sara asked, sitting at the head of the table, all eyes on her.

"Yes," Mr. Bark said.

"That's a shame." She cleared her throat, glancing around. "What are we supposed to do first?"

"I'm the sergeant at arms," The Rock said. "I have to call the meeting to order."

"Do it," Sara said.

The Rock stood and smashed his gavel on a wooden block and mumbled a few lines about the date and the time. Sara thought it a pathetic comment on student councils across the land that the sergeant at arms was an elected position. The Rock sat back down.

"Can I begin?" Sara asked. No one moved to stop her. "All right, I want this meeting to be short. I haven't eaten yet. I want all our meetings to be short, no longer than ten minutes."

"Sara," Mr. Bark said, interrupting. "That is ridiculous. A lot has to be accomplished during these meetings. Ten minutes is not enough time. But we don't want to keep you from eating. We offer a class here at Tabb called leadership. All the students in this room, except you, are in that class. Of course, we understand you did not expect to be nominated. For that reason, the faculty would be happy to rearrange your schedule so that you may join the class. That way we can take care of business during leadership and you can have the majority of your lunches free."

"Does leadership replace political science as a requirement?" Sara asked.

"No, it doesn't," Mr. Bark said.

"Then I don't want my schedule rearranged."

"Be serious—" Mr. Bark began.

"Rocky," Sara interrupted.

"I'm called The Rock."

"Whatever. Don't I have to recognize someone before they can speak?"

The Rock nodded. "It's in the bylaws."

"Mr. Bark," Sara said. "I don't recognize you. I'll tell you when I do." She glanced at her notes on the financial papers Mr. Bark had given her to review. "Let's get going. First, we're broke. We have a sum total of nineteen hundred and sixty-two dollars and thirteen cents in our activities account. With this we're supposed to put on both the Sadie Hawkins and the homecoming dances in the fall quarter. Now the senior class controls homecoming—and I'll get to that in a second—but the juniors are supposed to take care of Sadie Hawkins. Who's junior class president?"

A thin Japanese girl on her near right raised her hand. "I am."

"If I give you half of what we've got," Sara said. "Can you book a band, print up tickets, buy a truckload full of hay, and do whatever else you need to get this thing going?"

The girl hesitated. "I don't know everything involved."

"It's a question of cash flow. Figure out approximately how many people will attend, how much you'll have to spend to keep them happy. Then decide on a ticket price. The grand or so I'll give you will be to get you started until you can start collecting money. Do you understand?"

"Yes."

"Can you do it? I don't want to have to think about it."

The girl nodded. "The junior officers will take care of it."

"Good. We're making progress. Let's discuss homecoming. I think we should cancel it this year."

Now they were really staring at her. Clair—sitting to her left and looking sickeningly gorgeous—protested. "Are you out of your mind? It's the biggest event of the year."

"I have to recognize you," The Rock said. "Can I?"

"Yeah, she's recognized," Sara said, leaning toward Clair. "What do you mean it's the biggest event of the year? For you maybe, and four other *princesses* in the school. But for the rest of us slobs it's just another occasion to have dirt rubbed in our faces. So we're not as pretty as you? Whoever said good looks make a good person? Look at history. It's full of ugly kings and queens. Look at all the suffering that's gone on— Wait a second. Never mind. If the kings and queens had all been good-looking, it probably would have been worse. Let's get back to the issue. How many dances do we really need? Last year at Mesa, I never went to a single one. We already have Sadie Hawkins. I say that's enough. The alumni won't be coming back, anyway. I went to the game last Friday. I felt like leaving after the first quarter. What a bunch of clods."

Bill Skater raised his hand. "Can I speak?"

Sara sat back. "Rocky, recognize our quarterback."

The Rock did so. Bill stood, and Sara had to admit he had an imposing physique. She could see Jessica's reasons for wanting to get him alone in a dark and secluded spot. She wondered if perhaps she should have skipped the clods part.

"I don't think you have any right to knock our football team," he said. "One game doesn't mean nothing. Last year, the Super Bowl champs lost their first four games. And they ended up with the gold ring."

"Yeah," The Rock said.

"But that's not what I want to talk about," Bill went on. "I'm the treasurer. I've looked at our books, too, and I think we can afford homecoming. How much money do we need, anyway? It doesn't have to be that fancy. Homecoming is a tradition. Traditions are important. They're what makes this country great." He sat down.

"Yeah," Clair said. "Just because no one's going to vote you onto the homecoming court doesn't mean you've got to spoil it for the rest of us."

"What officer are you?" Sara asked.

"I'm vice-president," Clair said proudly.

"You were running for president. How did you get nominated for vice-president?"

Clair frowned. "I don't know."

Sara sighed. "I should have you all shot." The whole gang went to protest. Sara raised her hand. "All right, we'll keep homecoming. But we can't have it in the next few weeks, and I don't care what our treasurer says. We simply don't have the money. We're going to have to raise it somehow, and to do that, we need time. Let's have it during basketball season."

"That's absurd," Clair exploded. "Homecoming is always during football season. You can't change that."

"Why not?"

"Because you can't, that's why."

Sara strummed her fingers on top of the table. "I

will give you another reason why it must be post-poned. If the elections are held in the next couple of weeks, the girls from Mesa won't stand a chance of being nominated to the court. Transfers from Mesa like myself make up only a quarter of the student body. Hardly anyone who was originally from Tabb knows us. It wouldn't be fair."

Clair grinned. "Does Mesa have anyone we would vote for if we knew them ten years?"

The group giggled. Sara leaned toward Clair again. "Jessica Hart—remember that name. When the final count comes in, pimple brain, you won't be smiling."

Uncertain, Clair turned to Bill. "Who?" she whispered.

Bill nodded. "I've met her. She's pretty."

"How pretty?"

Bill shrugged.

"Rocky?" Sara said.

He pounded his gavel. "Order in the council."

Mr. Smith, the principal, raised his hand. "May I speak?"

"I recognize you myself," Sara said.

He stood. An older man close to retirement, he always wore—no matter what the weather—tailored three-piece suits. He had a faint English accent and was know for his exquisite manners.

"What you people decide is, of course, strictly up to you," he began. "But I would like to say that, in my opinion, Sara has made a persuasive argument for a postponement. This is, however, not the reason for my interruption. I was curious, Sara, how you plan on raising funds for homecoming outside of ticket sales and the like?"

"I don't know, maybe we can have a raffle."

Claire scowled. "This isn't a church. What are we going to raffle? A new TV set?"

Sara smiled faintly. "Maybe your body."

There followed cries of outrage and protest, plus plenty of good laughter. In the midst of it all—especially when Clair called for a presidential impeachment—Sara realized she was having fun. The remainder of the meeting—she let it run twenty minutes—passed quickly. It was decided homecoming could wait until winter. Naturally, she didn't recognize the vote of anyone who thought different.

Sara caught up with the principal in the hallway afterward. "Excuse me, Mr. Smith?"

He turned. "Ah, Sara, you're a strong-willed young lady. You've put a spark back into the council that's been missing for a number of years. But a word of advice from an old gentleman. In the future, please watch the personality attacks. I realize you say all those things in the spirit of jest, but as you must know, not everyone shares your sense of humor."

"I'll remember that, sir. Could I ask a favor of you?"

"Certainly."

She told him about Russ Desmond's expulsion from the cross-country team and the reason behind it. When she had finished, he said, "Russ is one of our finest athletes. It sounds like a misunderstanding that can easily be patched up. I'll have a word with Coach Campbell."

"Thanks a lot. I appreciate it."

"I do have a piece of bad news for you. It doesn't have to be taken care of immediately by the student council, but we have a soft drink machine that needs to be replaced. The accountants at the school district refuse to cover the cost. Apparently, one or more students had the bad sense to tip the machine over. It can't even be repaired."

Sara shook her head. "The barbarians."

113

CHAPTER NINE

Stepping onto the track near the runners, Jessica had to shield her eyes from the sun. Heat radiated in rippling waves off the ground over her bare legs. She couldn't imagine how anyone could run three miles on a day like this.

"They should postpone their race till evening," Alice said, wiping the sweat from her brow. "They'll get heat stroke in this."

"Maybe it'll rain," Sara said. There wasn't a cloud in the sky. She pointed toward the shadow cast by the scoreboard. "Let's go over there."

"Where's Polly?" Jessica asked.

"She said she was stopping for a drink," Alice said.

"Not a bad idea," Jessica said, turning to Sara. "See Russ?"

"No."

"You haven't even looked for him," Jessica said. "You've got to tell him you're here."

"I'm under no contractual obligation to do so," Sara said.

"Why wouldn't you?"

"He's here to run a race. Why should I bug him?"

"You're just afraid he won't remember you," Jessica said.

"You're right, I should have him knock me down again in case he's forgotten," Sara snapped. "Get off my case, Jessie. If he wants to talk to me, he can come over and talk to me."

"Sorry," Jessica muttered, surprised at her tone. Sara was usually about as sensitive to personal remarks as a brick wall.

They reached the shade and sat down. The grass tickled Jessica's legs. Alice continued to wipe at her head, the sweat literally pouring off her. "Are you all right?" Jessie asked.

Alice smiled quickly. "I'm fine, just glad I'm not running."

"But you were sick, weren't you? You didn't come in Monday or Tuesday."

Alice found a tiny yellow flower, plucked it. "I was painting."

"What?" Jessica said.

Alice threw her flower into the air, watched it fall directly to the ground. No breeze. "The blue wind."

"Really? Sounds interesting," Jessica said. "You'll have to show me. Hey, what are you doing this weekend? Want to go to the beach?"

"I'm painting."

"Couldn't you set it aside for a few hours."

"I've got to finish it."

"That's too bad." Jessica paused. "I'm going to the movies Saturday night. You won't believe it, I asked the guy. His name's Michael Olson."

Alice nodded slowly, leaning back, looking up into the clear sky. "Polly told me. That's neat that you found—someone you like."

"We're just friends. He's going to help me with

115

chemistry. That reminds me, where's that fantastic guy you were going to introduce me to?''

Alice lay down, closed her eyes. "Ask me after your date." She yawned. "I could go to sleep here and never wake up."

Jessica patted her arm. "You go ahead and rest."

Polly reappeared a few minutes later. Seconds before she reached them, however, Sara nodded in the direction of the stadium ramp. "That's him over there with the shaggy brown hair, the muscles," she said.

Jessica cupped her hand over her eyes again. "He looks tough."

"You don't like him?"

"I didn't say that. He's very attractive." He belonged in a black leather jacket on the back of a motorcycle. "He's the one who stopped that black guy from killing that football player?"

"Yeah," Sara said. "So what do you think?"

"I just told you," Jessica said. "He's attractive."

"Attractive. Phonies on TV are attractive. Do you like him?"

"Yes, I *really* like him. He's totally bitchin'," Jessica said.

"Shut up. I was only asking."

Polly waved. "What are you guys doing over here? They start and finish by the bleachers. Come on, let's move. What's Alice doing?"

"Dreaming," Alice whispered, her eyes still closed.

"She's taking a nap," Jessica said. "Sara wants to stay here in the shade."

Polly plopped down beside them, her face flushed with blood. "You won't believe who I was just talking to. Russ Desmond. He—"

"Shut up," Sara said.

Polly looked to Jessica. "What did I say?"

"It's the heat," Jessica said.

They stood—except for Alice, who appeared to have caught an early train to sleepyland—for the start of the race. The bang of the gun echoed off the mostly deserted stands. In a colorful jumbled herd—Russ lost in the center—the runners circled the track and vanished out the gate. "That's exciting," Jessica remarked. "What happens now?"

"We wait till they come back," Polly said.

Jessica preferred races where she got to see the runners running. She contemplated joining Alice in sleep on the grass.

Fifteen minutes later Russ reappeared, coming up the ramp. He had company, a short Japanese fellow clad in green dogging his heels. A cheer went up from the people gathered near the finish. Jessica leapt to her feet, her interest level taking a sharp upward climb. It was going to be close.

"Come on, Russ!" she yelled.

Russ accelerated sharply as he hit the track, opening up a ten-yard lead. He added another five yards as he went into the curve of the track, momentarily heading away from the finish but quickly approaching their vantage spot. Jessica poked Sara in the ribs.

"Cheer."

"Shh," Sara said, intent upon the race.

"Shout his name," Jessica said.

"Shh."

"Go!" Jessica yelled with Polly.

"Damn," Sara muttered. With a surge of his own, the Japanese guy had cut his lead in half. "Russ!!" Sara cried.

At the sound of her voice, he twisted his head toward them. He even raised his hand, shielding his eyes to see better. Then his left foot stepped onto the slightly upraised narrow cement strip that circled the inside of the track. The rhythm of his stride faltered;

117

he practically tripped. When he had recovered, the Japanese guy was ten yards in front. Russ went after him.

"Go!" they screamed.

He lost by inches. Maybe he would have lost, anyway, without the stumble. His competitor obviously had a powerful kick. Jessica told Sara as much. Sara would have none of it.

"I should have kept my mouth shut," she said. "Two races, two screw-ups."

"But it sure was exciting," Alice remarked, still on the ground, fresh from her snooze.

"What makes you think he was looking for you?" Polly asked Sara. "He could have been looking for me."

Jessica expected Sara to explode. Sara, however, ignored Polly completely. "Let's get out of here," she said.

"No, you should congratulate him on his effort," Jessica said. "I'll go with you."

Sara surprised her again. His loss seemed to have depressed her. "All right."

"I'm coming, too," Polly said.

"No," Jessica said. "Stay here. Stay with Alice."

"Why should I?"

"Because I'm asking you to. Please?"

Polly gave in reluctantly. Jessica and Sara approached the gang at the finish slowly, watching as the winner embraced Russ, hanging back for a few minutes while the coach and several of the other runners spoke to him about the race. Finally he separated himself from them and grabbed a can from the ice chest, heading for the shade behind the bleachers.

"You want to talk to him alone?" Jessica asked as they followed after him.

"No."

He must have been totally exhausted. Sitting with his back to a wooden plank, he didn't notice them coming. He had a beer in his hand, Jessica realized. Quite an ice chest they had here. Or else he filled it with his own private stock.

"Hi," Sara said.

He glanced up briefly. "Hi."

"This is my friend, Jessie."

Russ grunted. Sara looked at Jessica, uncertain. "That was a great race you ran," Jessica said quickly. His rough edges were more apparent up close, and yet, he also seemed somehow younger, more of a boy than she had thought from a distance.

"I've run better." He took a slug of beer, his eyes wandering to the baseball field.

"It's a shame you lost," Jessica said.

"You win some, you lose some."

"I didn't mean to distract you," Sara said.

Russ belched. "Hey, you got my axe?"

Sara paused. "What?"

"My axe. You took it the other night."

"No, I didn't."

"I need it back. It belongs to the store where I work."

"I don't have your axe."

"What did you do with it?"

"Nothing. I don't have it."

"What are you talking about?"

"What are *you* talking about?"

Russ looked vaguely annoyed. "You know, you're a weird girl."

Sara sucked in a sharp breath. "I'm weird? I'm weird? I'm not the one who's worried about some goddamn axe that he thinks he's lost."

He sharpened his tone. "I didn't lose it. You took it."

"Why would I take it?"

"You didn't want me to chop down the tree."

"What tree?"

Russ rubbed his head, growing tired of the whole discussion. "What are you doing here?" he muttered.

Sara chuckled. "I came over so *you* could thank *me* for getting you reinstated on the cross-country team."

"Huh?"

"In case you didn't know, I'm the school president. It was I who talked to the school principal. It was I who made it possible for you to run today."

She'd caught his attention. "No kidding?"

Sara nodded. "You better believe it."

He had a short attention span. He finished his can, crumpled it up in one hand, and threw it aside. "You shouldn't have bothered."

She stared at him for a long moment, and Jessica was just thankful Sara didn't have the missing axe in her hands. She probably wouldn't have killed him, but she might have taken a foot off. As it was, she turned and stalked off. Russ observed her departure with mild surprise. "Is it that time of month or what?" he asked.

"I think you might have hurt her feelings," Jessica said diplomatically.

"Oh, really?" he said innocently. "Well, I didn't mean to. Tell her I'm sorry."

Jessica knelt by his side. "This is probably none of my business, but do you like Sara?"

"Huh?"

"When she shouted for you in the race, I couldn't help noticing how you looked over. I was wondering if you liked her?"

"Yeah, she's all right. She's got a temper, though. God."

"Would you want to go out with her?"

"Where?"

"Anywhere, you know, like on a date?"

"I don't know. I guess."

She supposed that would have to do in place of yes. "Are you busy tomorrow night?"

"No."

Jessica took a pen and paper from her purse. It would be hopeless to give him Sara's number. He would only lose it. "I'll tell you what. Come over to my house tomorrow at six. Sara will be there. You can pick her up and the two of you can go out to dinner. How's that sound?"

"I don't know where you live."

"I'll draw you a map. Will you come?"

He shrugged. "All right. As long as she gives me back my axe."

CHAPTER TEN

Michael was no expert when it came to dressing for a date. Part of the reason, he supposed, was he had never gone on a date before. The other problem was his lack of nice clothes. He finally settled on a pair of gray slacks and a white shirt. He figured he was playing it safe. Bubba said he looked like an altar boy.

The three of them—Michael, Bubba, and Nick—were spending the last minutes before the *Big Night* in Michael's house. Bubba only lived around the block, and of course Nick had had to come over for the car. Michael's mom had already left for the weekend. Her current boyfriend, Daniel Stevens, owned a condo by the beach. Michael liked the man. Mr. Stevens taught music at UC-Irvine. He had an easygoing manner and treated his mother like gold. Michael suspected his mom liked him, too. Maybe this one would work out. She deserved someone nice.

"Did any of you go to the game last night?" Michael asked, sitting on his bed, sipping a lemonade. Nick—he couldn't seem to relax—had glued himself to the far wall. And Bubba was at the desk in front of the mirror, trying on a bag full of garish forties ties his gangster uncle had left him in a will.

"I didn't," Nick said.

"We got stomped: thirty-seven to fourteen," Bubba said. "There's a rumor circulating that Bill Skater's quarterback days are over."

"Did you start the rumor?" Michael asked.

"I did, but it's gathering momentum. I've also started a Draft Russ Desmond campaign, whether he wants to play or not." He turned away from the mirror. "What do you think of this one?"

Not only was it a depressing brandy-red color, it had a dime-size hole in the center. "It's awful," Michael said.

"That looks like a bullet hole," Nick said.

Bubba nodded. "My uncle was wearing it when he got wasted." He tightened the collar. "Clair will love it."

"What did Clair say when you told her she had to drive?" Michael asked.

"We'll see," Bubba said, reaching for the phone. He dialed the number from memory. She answered on the second ring. "Clair? This is Bubba. How are you doing? . . . Hey, that's great. I can hardly wait myself. But I've got a small problem. You know Michael Olson? . . . Yeah, he sure is smart. He's going out with Jessica Hart tonight. . . . What? No, she's cool. Never mind what you've heard. Anyway, he has to borrow my car. Could you pick me up? . . . What a sweetheart! Let me give you my address."

He chit-chatted a minute longer before signing off. "She loves me," he said as he put down the phone.

"Do you swear you don't have those tickets?" Michael asked.

"U2 played their final L.A. show last night. How could I have tickets?"

"What did she say about Jessie?"

"She called her a stuck-up bitch. Don't take it personally. It's only because Jessie's pretty. Pretty girls always hate other pretty girls. It's biological."

Nick ventured away from the wall. "I better get going." He had a long face.

"Hey, loosen up, Nick," Bubba said. "You're just going out with her. You don't have to kill her afterward."

Michael stood, setting down his lemonade. "Are you worried because she's having you pick her up at the library?"

Nick looked at the floor. "I don't know, when I think about it, maybe she's ashamed of me."

"She's probably just worried her dad will blow your head off when he sees how dark you are," Bubba said sympathetically.

Nick smiled faintly. "Yeah, that must be it."

Michael escorted Nick to the front door. "I filled the car with gas this afternoon," he said. "The air conditioner works, but the window's usually a better bet. And forget about the radio. It only gets AM."

"Thanks, Mike."

"The car's ten years old. It's no big favor."

Nick went to touch his shoulder, hesitated. "I mean, thanks for everything. You're a real friend. Where I come from, you learn to appreciate your friends. Anytime you need a favor, no matter what it is, I'll be there for you."

Michael was touched by the sentiment. "You just have yourself a good time."

Nick promised him he would. Michael watched him drive off, and was heading back to his room when Kats pulled up. Kats drove an old Mustang that never needed an oil change; it leaked a quart a week. "Don't park that thing in the driveway!" Michael called.

"You let that black dude take your car?" Kats asked a minute later, after having stowed his heap out of sight around the corner. He had obviously just come from work. He needed a bath. "You must be out of your mind, Mike."

Michael ignored the comment—people did that all the time with Kats—fetched him a glass of lemonade, and told him not to sit on anything. Bubba came out of the bedroom with a box of condoms in his hands.

"You sure you don't want at least one of these?" he asked.

"That's all right, you might need the whole box," Michael said.

Bubba nodded. "I did use a whole box once. Lost three pounds that night. Gained it right back, though. It was mostly water."

Michael groaned. "If you're going to talk like that, we better go in the bathroom."

"Don't be a prude. They advertise condoms on national television. Safe sex, all that stuff." Bubba pulled one from the box, offered it to him. "Come on, she'll thank you for it afterward."

"Give it to Kats."

Kats was excited. "How many of those have you got to wear?"

Bubba glanced at Kats's filthy fingernails. "You? Eleven."

Michael pointed to the orange envelope with Jessica's address on it. "Kats, hand me that paper on the oven, would you?"

Kats picked the invitation up, stopped to read it. He was nosy on top of everything else. His grin widened. "Polly and Alice McCoy! They come into the station all the time. Always pay with a gold credit card. You know them, Mike? Are they having a party? I'd like to go to that. Wooh, that Alice sure is a tasty number."

125

Michael took a step forward, snapped the invitation from Kats's hand. "Shut up. You have to be invited. You can't come."

"Hey, Mike," Bubba said. "Cool down."

Michael realized he was overreacting. "Sorry."

Kats stared at him a moment, his black eyes strangely flat. Then he grinned again. "I bet you were just afraid I'd break in carrying my gun, hey, Mike?"

Michael folded the invitation, put it in his back pocket, out of sight. He remembered that gun all too well. "Yeah, I guess, something like that."

He had asked Jessica yesterday if she'd like to get a bite to eat before the movie. She had said sure. He was supposed to pick her up at six-thirty. He would be early if he left now, but suddenly he wanted to get out of the house, get away from the others. He told them he had to hit the road. Bubba left with Kats in the dripping Mustang.

Michael was familiar with Jessica's neighborhood. And although he had never been to the McCoy residence, he knew Alice lived around the block from Jessica; he had both addresses on the invitation. Cruising down the road in Bubba's Jaguar, he decided to swing by and say hello to his favorite artist.

He had expected a huge house. He wasn't disappointed. You could use up a lot of gas, he thought, going up a driveway like this every day; it was as long as a football field. He parked beside a silver gray Mercedes, climbed out.

An elderly lady answered the door. He assumed she was the guardian aunt Alice talked about. Her posture was terrible; in better years, she must have been half a foot taller. She was one of those old ladies it was hard to imagine had ever been young. She had a sweet smile, however, which reminded him of Alice's. Parents and relatives always smiled when they saw him. As Bubba had observed, he had that altar boy aura.

"Is Alice here?"

"She's around back. Are you a friend from school?"

"Yeah, I'm Michael Olson." He offered his hand. She shook it feebly.

"Alice has told me about you. Please come in."

They had cream-colored carpet, deep and soft. The living room cathedral ceiling went way up; twin tinted skylights spread a faint rainbow of color over the elegant contemporary furniture and towering fireplace. The place was spotless. *They'd better lay down protective sheets for the party,* he thought. The aunt pointed toward a sliding glass door. "You'll find her near the rose bushes."

"Thank you. Is Polly here?"

"She's at a friend's."

The pool was large even for a house as big as this one. It was not, however, exotically shaped, simply rectangular. Mr. or Mrs. McCoy had probably enjoyed swimming laps.

Alice had set up her easel in the corner of the yard, between the wall of the house and the beginnings of an exotic garden of flowers, bushes, and trees that stretched perhaps fifty yards to a tall adobe brick wall. The McCoys could do all the shouting they liked and their neighbors wouldn't even know about it.

An overhang from the second-story roof cast a shadow over her spot. She had compensated by erecting a silver-dished lamp behind her right shoulder. He thought the arrangement unusual since she could have painted practically anywhere else in the yard and enjoyed direct sunlight. Perhaps the strange mixture of artificial and natural lighting was what suited her mood best. Although he could scarcely see the paint-

127

ing, her work in progress appeared—from the colors—
to have a distinct surreal quality.

He thought how content she seemed with a brush in
her left hand, a song on her lips. Maybe she was in the
middle of a creative high. He decided not to interrupt
her, after all. He circled around to the other side of
the house and climbed back in the Jaguar. The aunt
would probably wonder what had become of him.

It hit him then, hard as a rock, that he was going to
pick up Jessica. *Jessie!* The nervousness came quick,
but also, an exhilarating joy. This could be the start of
something. She could fall in love with him. It was
theoretically possible.

He drove around the block, parked in the street in
front of her house. Ringing the doorbell and waiting
for her to answer, he aged five years.

When the doorbell rang, Jessica was upstairs in her
bedroom with Sara and Polly, trying on earrings. She
sent Polly down to answer it. "If it's Michael, tell him
I'll be down in a minute. Offer him a Coke."

"What if it's Russ?" Polly asked.

Jessica glanced at Sara. "Give him a beer," she
said.

When Polly had left, Sara went to the bedroom door
and peeked out. "It's Mike," she said a moment later,
disappointed.

"He'll be here, Sara. He's only a few minutes late."

"Thirty-two minutes is not a few."

"Guys have a different sense of time than girls."

"Are you absolutely positively sure it was his idea
to go out?"

"Yes."

"You're lying. You talked him into it."

"He likes you. He told me so."

"Did he say that? What were his exact words?"

"He said you were an all-right girl." She decided against any earrings at all. They were just going out for fun, after all. She turned to Sara. "Look, why don't you call him? He may have gotten lost."

"Right, it'll be a snap reaching him on his car phone."

"You've got a point there. Maybe you could talk to his mom. I'm sure their number is listed. She could tell you when he left."

Sara folded her arms across her chest. She'd broken from tradition and put on a beautiful white dress. "I'm not talking to his mom."

Jessica squeezed Sara's arm. "Be patient. He'll be here. Now, I've got to go. Wish me a good time."

"Have a good time," Sara grumbled.

"Don't you want to come down and say hi to Michael?"

Sara plopped on the bed. "No. I hate men. All of them."

Michael was sitting on the couch with Polly when Jessica entered the living room. He stood up quickly when he saw her and smiled. His gray slacks and white shirt looked a bit plain next to her bright yellow pants and silky green blouse, but who gave a damn? The degree of her pleasure at seeing him again surprised her. He had such lovely black eyes.

"You look nice," he said casually, stepping toward her. On impulse, she gave him a quick hug.

"Thanks, so do you." His arms felt strong beneath his shirt. She took a step back. "Did you have any trouble finding the place?"

"No."

"Where are my manners? Have you met Polly?"

"I met Mike last year," Polly said. "He's a good friend of Alice's."

Jessica stopped, frowned. "You are? Alice didn't tell me that."

Michael was watching her. "She's a nice girl."

"Alice? She's a doll." Jessica picked her purse off the TV. "I'd introduce you to my parents, but they went out for dinner. Which reminds me, where do you want to eat? Remember, I'm paying."

He mentioned a local restaurant—one of her favorites—but insisted it would be his treat. She told him they could argue about it when the bill came.

As she was leaving, she remembered that Maria would be coming over later to spend the night. All this last week, since Maria had helped her on the quiz, they had begun to talk more, outside of class as well as during chemistry lab. Maria was a different sort of friend for Jessica. She was serious, someone who weighed every word before speaking it. She appeared totally uninterested in local gossip, and yet she was fun to be around. She had a quiet dignity that Jessica found inspiring.

On Thursday Maria had admitted she had a problem. Nick Grutler, the tall black guy, had asked her out. She wanted to go; she had, in fact, told him she would. But her parents would kill her if they found out. They weren't prejudiced, she said, just *extremely* conservative. She had told Nick to pick her up at the library, but she knew that when he dropped her off at home, her parents would be awake and waiting. She didn't know what to do.

To Jessica, the solution was obvious. Spend the night at her house. The offer had delighted Maria. To further insure that Maria's parents did not learn of the date, Jessica had called Friday afternoon after the cross-country race and had casually spoken to Mrs. Gonzales about Maria's coming over. The lady had sounded pleased her daughter had made such an upstanding friend. You just had to know how to handle parents.

"Are you going to hang around for a while?" she asked Polly. "I forgot to tell my mom and dad about Maria spending the night."

"I might stay for a while."

"Until Russ shows up, right?" Polly started to get mad. "Don't say it. If you do leave before they get back, could you leave them a note for me?"

"Sure, Jessie. I hope you two have fun."

Michael probably was going to think she was a jerk. The second they left the house, she asked if they could stop at the nearest gas station. "I have to make a call," she explained.

"Your house phones aren't working?"

"Yeah."

They stopped at an Exxon not far away. Excusing herself, she shut herself in the booth and rang information. There were three Desmonds. The first one didn't have a Russ. The second—it sounded like his dad—said he'd go get him. Russ didn't seem all that wide-awake when he came on the line.

"Hello?"

"Hi, Russ, this is Jessica Hart. Remember me?"

"Yeah."

Jessica gestured to Michael that she would be off in a moment. "Russ, where are you? Don't you remember you were supposed to go out with Sara tonight?"

He yawned. "It was tonight?"

Jessica wondered if she should stop where she was. Chances were, Sara would eventually kill a guy like this. "Yeah, how could you forget?"

"I don't know. Can I come tomorrow? I'm watching *Star Trek*."

"No, you can't come tomorrow. Sara's waiting for

you at my house this minute. She's all dressed up.
You get over there right away."

"Right now? I'm hungry."

"You made a date, Russ. You should keep it. Do
you still have that map I drew you?"

"I think so."

"Good. Now whatever you do, don't tell her I
called. All right?"

"All right."

Nick's worst nightmare was coming true. They were
in the car together, driving down the road, and they
had absolutely nothing to say to each other. He didn't
even know where he was taking her. He had assumed
she would suggest a place she wanted to eat, the movie
she wanted to see. Now he suspected she was waiting
for him to make the decision. Unfortunately, he hardly
knew the area. He didn't want to risk taking her to the
local doghouse. The silence between them dragged on
and on.

"How was the library?" he asked finally.

"Fine."

"Did you get a lot of homework done?"

"I should have done more. What did you do today?"

"I worked at the store in the morning. Then I just
hung out."

"Oh."

They'd had a couple of other mini-conversations
like this. They had also ended with "oh." The word
could be used in practically any situation. Nick worried that they would keep coming back to it all night.
He felt he had to say something different, something
to break them out of their rut. Actually, he wanted to
tell her how happy he was that she had agreed to go
out with him, but since he was feeling rather miserable

at the moment, he was afraid it would come out sounding insincere. He decided on a different tact.

"How do you feel?" he asked.

"Good."

"That's good."

"How do you feel?"

"Good. I mean, I'm OK."

"Is something wrong?" she asked.

"No. Why do you ask?"

"No reason. I was just asking."

"Oh."

See—now he had said it. He was seriously debating whether he should give up right then and there and take her home when he noticed her staring at him. "What is it?" he asked.

"You're mad at me, aren't you?"

"Why would I be mad? I'm not mad."

"I didn't invite you to my house."

"That's all right. You were working at the library."

"That didn't fool you, Nick."

Her saying his name—on top of her confession—seemed to loosen something in the air. At home, he seldom heard his name. He didn't think his dad had said it in the last five years. "Is it your parents?" he asked.

She nodded. "They don't know I'm out with you."

"They don't let you date?"

She hesitated. "Not exactly."

"Oh." The light turned red. Stopping, he rolled down the window. The outside air had cooled significantly. They must be getting close to the beach. Naturally, what she said did not surprise him. That was the thing about being one of the few blacks in the neighborhood—you got used to everything. "Do you feel guilty?"

"No. I'm not doing anything wrong."

"But I could be getting you into trouble?"

"You won't. I'm spending the night at a friend's."

It stung to hear how she'd had to set everything up beforehand. Maybe he was mad at her, a little. "Does this friend have parents?" he asked. "You know, they might see me accidentally."

She turned toward him. "I'm sorry."

The regret came swift. "No, Maria, I shouldn't have said that."

"My parents are good people. They just feel they have to be cautious. They haven't had easy lives."

He waited till the light turned green, then drove across the street and parked near the curve. Behind Maria, through a patch in the bushes along the sidewalk, he saw a blue slice of ocean, the warm brown of sand. He turned off the engine. "And you feel you have to be cautious, too, right?"

She nodded, watching him.

"Why?"

"I just have to be."

"Then what are you doing with me?"

She didn't answer, but continued to stare. She seemed scared, not of him, but of what he might say. He said it anyway. "You and your parents are illegal aliens, aren't you?"

She trembled, ever so slightly. "Yes," she whispered.

"There were lots in my old neighborhood."

She nodded. "I knew."

"What?"

"You would know. When I met you at the soda machines, you looked like someone—who knew who didn't belong."

He chuckled. "I suppose a bloody head might give someone that idea." Then he got serious. "What's the big crime? They've loosened the laws. Stay here a few years and they'll make you a citizen.''

"That's not how it works. We got here after the amnesty deadline. In Washington there's talk about changing the requirements, but until then we could be sent home anytime."

"How did you get registered at school?"

"My dad paid this man some money. He made me a phony birth certificate."

"How long have you been in the country?"

"Almost two years. We're from El Salvador."

"How is it there?"

She tensed. "Not good. I like it better here." She gently touched his knee. He could not remember when he had last been touched by a female. Probably by his mom, before she had split eight years ago. "I'd rather not talk about it, if you don't mind? I worry too much about it as it is."

"What would you like to do?"

She brightened. "Eat. I'm starving. You don't know where you're going, do you?"

He smiled. "No."

She told him about a Mexican restaurant next to the pier. Nick restarted the car. She hadn't asked him to keep her secret. She'd automatically trusted him to do so. He was glad.

Russ had half a roast beef sandwich in his hand when Sara answered the door, the other half in his mouth. "Sorry I'm late," he mumbled, chewing.

He had on blue jeans, a torn red T-shirt, and sandals. Sara silently cursed Jessica for talking her into dressing up. He hadn't even combed his hair. "Did you have trouble finding the place?" she asked diplomatically.

"No."

Polly popped her head out the side of the door. "Hi, Russ! How are you doing?"

He grinned. "Hanging in there, babe. How are you?"

Sara pushed Polly out of the way. "We've got to go. Remember to feed the cat." She stepped outside, shutting the door in Polly's face. That girl only liked a guy when he belonged to someone else. "Where's your car?"

"I don't have a car. I've got a truck. It's right there."

Sara grimaced. It looked like he used it for hauling. She pointed to the mound of grass piled in the back. "Do you keep a cow, or what?"

He didn't think that was funny. "My old man's a gardener. What's yours do?"

"He shuffles papers." He was a bank president.

"Does he use a truck to deliver them?"

Jessica had warned her to watch her mouth. Jessica said guys didn't appreciate being made fools of. "Ah, yeah."

"What do you want to do?" he asked as they walked toward his truck.

"I'm hungry."

He took another bite of his sandwich. "You haven't had dinner?"

"No. I thought we were going to eat together?"

"That's cool. Let's go to the McDonald's in the mall."

"The McDonald's?"

He opened the passenger door, and as he did so, she caught a whiff of his breath. The empty beer cans littering his front seat only confirmed her fears. "You've been drinking," she said.

"Is there a law against it? If you want, we can go to the Burger King instead."

"How many beers have you had?" Judging by his empties, he'd put away several six-packs; but that seemed unlikely.

"Why? I can drive."

"How many?"

"I can't remember."

"I'm driving." She held out her hand. He stared at it a moment before giving her the keys.

"Do you know how to drive a stick?"

"I learned on a stick," she said, reaching into the passenger side and removing what was left of a six-pack. "I'm putting these in the back, under the grass. I don't want some cop stopping and arresting us." As it was, her license was still in suspension.

"They'll get warm," he protested. "One of them's half-full."

"I don't care."

The driver's seat was encrusted not only with dirt, sweat, and more dead grass, but also had a dozen or so of those little thorny balls that get stuck on clothes at picnics. She looked down at her white dress, running her fingers over the clean smooth fabric. She'd bought it in Hollywood at a designer shop for big bucks. Then she looked over at Russ: food in his mouth, hair in his face, not much going on behind his eyes.

What the hell am I doing with this guy?

But it was right then that he showed the first trace of decency he had since their collision when he stopped during the race to see if she'd been hurt. Without her even asking, he pulled off his shirt and draped it over her seat. And sitting there naked from the waist up, his powerfully developed chest warm and brown in the evening sunlight, he seemed to her, if not perfect, at least worthy of consideration. She got in.

"You've got to watch the brakes," he said as she

fiddled with the clutch. King Kong could hardly have pressed the thing in.

"What's wrong with them?"

"They don't always work."

She stopped. "You can't be serious?"

He shrugged. "If you don't like it, let's take your car. That'll give me a chance to look in your trunk."

She didn't have her car; Jessica had picked her up. "What's in my trunk?"

"I think that's where you put my axe."

Sara leaned her head on the steering, totally reversing her opinion of a moment ago. "Jesus," she whispered.

Dinner had been fabulous. Probably because the restaurant overlooked the ocean, they'd both been in the mood for seafood; she'd had a shrimp salad, and Michael, swordfish. Although she was already stuffed, the pastry tray the waitress had brought by a moment ago was too much of a temptation. Fortunately, Michael promised to eat half the chocolate cake she had ordered. She was going to have to jog a few miles this weekend to make up for tonight. She didn't care. She was having a great time.

Initially, while thinking about the date that afternoon, she had worried she would come off seeming stupid, shallow. She had always done well in school, but since third grade, she had felt she was faking it. She got good grades, she thought, because she studied twice as much as anybody else. She saw herself as an overachiever and feared that one day, someday, she would be found out. Everyone would know she didn't really belong in the accelerated math class, or chemistry for that matter.

Yet rather than trying to hide her insecurity from the smartest guy around, she found herself confiding in him about it. She wasn't even sure why, other than that Michael was an excellent listener.

"I keep reading about the average GPAs of the kids who get into Stanford," she said. "And their SAT scores. They're so high! I'm not taking the test until December, and I've already bought a couple of those study guide books. I took a trial test a couple of nights ago. I won't tell you what I scored. Let's just say if I do as well on the real test, I'm going to save my dad a lot of money on tuition fees. I swear to God, sometimes I think I'm going to end up at the local junior college."

"What do you want to major in at Stanford?" he asked. He had taken a fancy to the candle on their table and was playfully running his fingers above the flame. She didn't doubt she had his full attention, however; he wasn't staring, but his eyes seldom wandered far from her face. Once again, she wondered how he saw her.

"My parents eventually want me to get into broadcasting. They tell me I've got the voice, the personality. They think a major in journalism, with a minor in communications, would give me a solid background. I know some of those girls on the news make a lot of money. What do you think?"

"I think I asked the wrong question."

She smiled. "What do you mean?"

He momentarily took his hand away from the candle, caught her eye. "You keep telling me what your parents want."

She started to answer, stopped. He'd hit pretty close to home with that one. "They are paying the bills," she muttered.

He backed off. "I didn't mean they were giving you bad advice. They obviously care a great deal about you."

"No, you're right. I need to hear this. I should major in what *I* want. It is my life, after all. But that's the problem. I don't know what I want. Being an anchorperson on TV looks glamorous. Everyone knows who you are. You're where the action is. But that's looking at it from the outside in. For all I know, I might hate it."

He nodded. "That's true. But if you really are interested, you probably could get a summer job at a TV station. You might only change lights, but at least you'd get a feel for the environment."

"That's an idea." She made a mental note to check on that.

"What about Stanford?"

"What about it? Don't you think it's a good school?"

"It's one of the best. Is that why you've chosen it?"

He'd caught her again. "My dad went to Stanford," she admitted. "I grew up browsing through his college yearbooks. I know all the sororities on campus, even the Stanford school song. I don't know, it's so hard to get into, I've always felt that if you graduated from Stanford, you would be one of the elite." She leaned forward. She really wanted his approval. "Does that sound like too snobbish a reason?"

He chuckled. "I'm the last person to ask."

"Why?"

" 'Cause I'm jealous. *I* won't be going to Stanford."

"Why not? You've got the grades. You'll probably get super-high SAT scores."

He looked down. "I can't afford it."

She had to remember that not everybody's dad made six figures a year. He must have borrowed the Jaguar for their date. "Couldn't you get a scholarship?"

He shrugged. She may have been embarrassing him. "It's a possibility, but I'd hate to be that far away from my mom. She sort of likes having me around."

He'd said nothing about his family. "Is your mom divorced?"

"Yeah."

"You don't have any brothers or sisters, do you?"

"No."

"Neither do I. I wish I did. I sort of envy Polly sometimes. She's got Alice." He glanced up suddenly. "What is it?"

"Nothing," he said.

"It really surprised me that you knew her. She never told me. When did you meet?"

"Last Christmas?"

"Really? Where?"

"At the store where I work. The Seven-Eleven on Western."

"I've been in there a couple of times. I never saw you. Is it a part-time job?"

"Fifty hours a week."

"Wow." He lived in a different world, she realized. He made money, carried his own weight. She charged everything, ran up the phone bill. And from what he said, he watched out for his mom, when all she did was fight with her parents about nothing. She lived such a superficial life.

But what can I do? I'm already spoiled.

She decided she couldn't possibly accept his help with chemistry. He undoubtedly had little time to himself.

She leaned over, blew out the candle beneath his hand. "Come on, Michael. We don't need the cake. I'm taking you to that movie I promised."

They called for the check. She put up a fight, but he insisted on paying. Out in the car, they checked a paper he'd brought. They couldn't make up their minds what to see and decided to head back to the mall near campus where they would have six shows to choose from.

Driving along Pacific Coast Highway, the salty air pouring in through the open windows, the sun setting over the water, they slipped into a quiet spell. Relaxing into the seat, she glanced over, studying his profile. For a moment she wished that it had been he who had asked her out, that this was a *real* date. He didn't have Bill Skater's startling blue eyes, his strong jaw. But his face was appealing, particularly now, with his dark eyes intent upon the road, his thoughts seemingly far away. And he had something else she liked. He was kind.

Twenty minutes later, while reviewing the movie posters outside the mall's theaters, they heard their names called.

"Maria!" she cried, turning.

"Hi, Nick," Michael said. "It's a small city."

They made an interesting couple. Maria couldn't have been five feet tall, and Nick had to be pushing six and a half. They were not holding hands, but Jessica noticed how close they stood, how their arms and sides brushed as they approached. She had been curious to meet Nick. She'd heard such contrasting stories: that he was a bloodthirsty maniac; that he had risked his life to protect Russ Desmond from a huge toppling mirror; that he had the strength of ten guys. Watching him now shaking Michael's hand, shyly saying hello to her, she marveled at his politeness.

They decided to team up. But if it was difficult for two to choose a movie, it was impossible for four. Not that they were each insisting their own personal taste be the deciding factor. On the contrary, Michael, Nick, and Maria refused to volunteer any preference, and Jessica didn't know what she wanted to see. They had time. They decided to have ice cream first.

They ran into Bubba and Clair inside the 31 Flavors.

Meeting him at the game, Jessica had thought Bubba a wonderful character, not someone she would like to get too close to, but a guy it would be nice to run into from time to time when she needed a taste of the extraordinary. He obviously had Sara's highly developed sense of self-confidence, as well as her wit. Yet he seemed somehow both more fun loving and more devious. She had been surprised to learn he had been a friend of Michael's for many years.

Bubba took charge of the introductions. When it was time for Jessica to formally meet Clair, Jessica found herself becoming defensive. She'd heard what Clair had said in the student council meeting about how all the female transfers from Mesa were dogs.

"Clair, this is someone you have to know," Bubba said, excited. "Miss Jessica Hart. She used to be a cheerleader at Mesa. The best they had, I've been told. Jessie, meet my pal, Clair Hilrey." He chuckled. "Clair *is* the best."

Clair blushed at Bubba's remark, remaining seated beside a half-consumed banana split. She had an overall flushed look, as if she had just been out in the sun, or exercising. A thin gold necklace glittered at her throat. Crossing her exquisite long legs, she offered her hand. "I've heard about you," she said sweetly. "I've been wanting to meet you."

Jessica shook her hand. She wondered what Clair was doing with short, fat Bubba, whether this meant Bill and she weren't a couple, anymore. She forced a smile. "I've seen you at the games."

"Yeah?"

"Cheering, you know." Who did this girl's hair?

Jessica wondered. That person should be doing her own.

Clair glanced at Bubba, giggled. "That's what we cheerleaders do here at Tabb."

"Yeah," Bubba said. "They're full of spirit. They never get tired. Hey, why don't you guys join us? We're going to go to the movies in a few minutes."

Michael and Nick didn't react to the suggestion one way or the other, although Maria did not seem particularly enthusiastic. The three of them appeared to be waiting for her decision. Clair smiled at her again, the fine lines of arrogance beautifully arranged around her wide, sensual mouth. Jessie almost felt as if Clair were challenging her to stay. *Come on, girl, see who all the boys start fawning over.* Jessica met her eyes. "That sounds like fun," she said.

They ate ice cream, lots of it, until they were all sick and groaning. Then they headed back to the theaters. They didn't have to worry about selecting a movie. Bubba did it for them. He'd read the reviews and heard the inside Hollywood buzz, he said, and they would be crazy to see anything else. It was something about a female vampire from outer space who didn't wear any clothes.

Michael had been right. It *was* a small city. They bumped into Sara and Russ next, standing in line for the same movie. Russ must have picked it; Jessica knew how much Sara hated anything sci-fi. Indeed, Sara didn't appear to be having a thrilling night. She pulled Jessica aside the first chance she got.

"I'm going nuts," she hissed, while the others talked together in line. "Do you know where he took me for dinner?"

"Where?"

"I'll let you guess. The menu was fabulous. We had a choice of hamburgers: single patty, double patty, cheese on top, and cheese on the bottom. Then we had our choice of shakes: vanilla, strawberry, chocolate. Of course, if you ordered the full dinner, you got complimentary french fries.''

"That sounds like McDonald's?"

"Very good. But dinner was the fun part. Before that, he let me take him for a scenic drive in his garbage truck. And guess what? Two local civil servants stopped us to point out the twenty bushels of dead grass we had flying out the back.''

"You were driving? Did they ask for your license?"

"That they did. Fortunately, my less than sober male companion ingeniously told them I had accidentally left it in the back before we had piled in the grass. The cops didn't mind. They told me to dig it out. They even helped me. And guess what they found?"

"More dead grass?"

"No. Beer. Alcohol. That stuff they sell to people after they are twenty-one years of age. They found three cans, and one of them was open. That's against the law, in case you didn't know.''

"Did you get a ticket?" Sara's license was already in suspension; another ticket and they would probably tear it up.

"No, I got arrested!"

"No!"

"I had to take a sobriety test. I had to walk in a straight line and breathe in a bag. And get this, all the while Russ—drunk out of his gord—got to sit there and watch!''

"Did you get a ticket?" she repeated. Sara had not been arrested.

"No, I got humiliated! Then I had to eat a greasy hamburger, which gave me indigestion. And now I've got to watch some goddamn flick about a blood-sucking pin-up." She glared in the direction of her date, fuming. "I wish the cops had given me a urine test. Then I could have thrown it in his face."

"But do you like him? Are you having fun?"

"Shut up. What are you guys going to see?"

"The same thing you are." Jessica noticed Clair fixing Michael's collar, her polished nails brushing the back of his neck. Bubba noticed, too, and didn't seem to care. Jessica couldn't say the same for herself.

Am I jealous? I can't be jealous. He's just a friend.

"Let's get back in line," she said.

Clair backed away from Michael the moment they returned. For the first time that night, Jessica took Michael's hand. Clair whispered something in Bubba's ear, causing him to laugh.

"What's up?" Michael asked innocently. Jessica pulled him close, squeezed the top of his arm, smiled.

"I am." Maybe, just maybe, he would be more than a friend.

The fireworks between Sara and Russ were not over. When Russ reached the ticket window, he discovered he didn't have enough money for two admissions. He asked Sara if she could spring for a few dollars. Sara stared at him for a long time before responding. Jessica silently hoped Sara was using the time to calm herself. She might just as well have been hoping for a gallon of gasoline to put out a fire.

"What?" Sara asked softly. "You want money from *me*? You want *me* to pay for *your* movie? Is that what *you* want?"

Poor Russ, he was looking right into the face of a volcano and he couldn't feel the heat. The girl behind the ticket window waited with an expression of infinite boredom. "Yeah," he said.

Sara took out her purse, opened it for all to see. She must have had forty bucks, in tens and fives, and plenty of change. She smiled when she saw the money, and Jessica shivered. It was a crooked smile Sara saved for special occasions, immediately before she exploded into a frenzy.

"Hey, why don't we make this my treat," Jessica said quickly, stepping up to the window, pulling out a twenty. "Why don't I—"

"She's got plenty of dough," Russ interrupted. He stretched his hand over to pluck a bill from Sara's purse. Sara held it out of reach. He frowned. "Hey, come on, we're holding up the line."

"No," Sara said.

"What do you mean, no?" Russ demanded.

"You didn't say please."

"Please what? Please give me a couple of bucks? Man, you're— All right, all right, please give me a couple of bucks."

Sara stopped smiling. "No."

"What do ya want to see?" the chick in the window finally asked. The people behind them began to stir.

Michael took out his wallet. "Russ, I could lend you a ten if you need—"

"No," Sara interrupted, her eyes fixed on Russ. "No one's loaning this buffoon a red penny."

Russ shook his head, disgusted. "You know what your problem is, girl? You're spoiled. You get everything handed to you on a platter. You've got no class."

Sara started to laugh, loud and high, like a hyena. She did this for maybe three seconds, then suddenly cut it off and poked a sharp finger into Russ's chest. "I have no class!" she screamed. "You're an hour late! Your truck smells like a cow stall! You practically get me thrown in jail, and now you're pinching money out of my purse!"

"That's telling him," Bubba said, enjoying the exchange. The others held back. It was too late, Jessica knew, to go back.

"My truck doesn't stink," Russ said indignantly. "And I'm not pinching your money. I'm just short is all. I didn't know I was going to have to pay for all this tonight."

Sara went to snap at him, stopped. Jessica began to feel faint. "What do you mean?" Sara asked quietly.

"I didn't know we were going out until your friend called me. If I'd known, I would have went—"

"Stop," Sara said. She glanced at her, spoke to Russ. "Jessie called you? When did Jessie call you?"

Russ lowered his head, realizing his mistake. "I don't know."

Sara nodded. "Jessie set this all up, didn't she? Yeah, that makes sense. You're being a jerk 'cause you don't want to be here. Well, I can understand that." She took a breath. "I'm sorry."

"What do ya want to see?" the girl asked again. She had the line down pat. Sara reached into her purse, threw all her money under the window.

"The vamp flick," she told her, glancing at the rest of them. "It's on me."

Then she left, in a hurry, and Jessica was not able to catch up to her until they were halfway across the mall, near the central fountain. Fortunately, none of the others followed. Sara was crying. Jessica would not have thought it possible.

"I didn't know this would happen," Jessica said. "I didn't know."

Sara didn't tell her to go away, didn't blame her. Removing a handkerchief from her bag, she slowly wiped away her tears, blew her nose. Jessica watched with a mixture of guilt and amazement. Who was this fragile creature? It couldn't be her best friend. That girl *never* cried, not in the twelve years she had known her. Sara looked at her with red eyes.

"I would call a cab, but I spent all my money," she said.

"I'll go get Michael. We'll give you a ride home. You stay here until I get back." She put her arm around her. "I really am sorry."

Sara smiled faintly, embarrassed. "This is stupid."

Jessica hugged her. "No, this just means you like him."

Michael met her midway between the theaters and the fountain. She explained how Sara would rather not have to see the others any more tonight. He understood immediately; he went for the car.

They drove to Jessica's house; Sara had planned to spend the night, anyway, and Jessica wanted to talk to her. Sara didn't say a word, except to thank Michael when she got out of the car. Jessica watched her hurry to the front door, disappear inside. She turned to Michael.

"I guess I still owe you a movie," she said.

"That's OK."

"You know, you're being awfully cool about all this. I think I would feel better if you were a little put out or something."

He played with the keys in the ignition. Now he wouldn't look at her, and for a moment she wondered if he was nervous. But he hadn't asked her out. He couldn't be thinking of kissing her good night.

What if I kissed him?

"Sara seemed pretty upset," he said, rolling down his window and placing his left elbow halfway outside. In the confines of the front seat, he had placed himself as far away from her as possible. She decided to take the hint. He didn't want her kisses. He probably just wanted to get back to see the movie. She couldn't blame him.

"Yeah, she is. I better go see her."

"OK." He glanced up the street. "I have some free time tomorrow evening, if you still need help with chemistry?"

He probably had to work all day, and would be exhausted when he got home. She would be stealing his own study time. "Oh, that, never mind. I've been reading the textbook like mad the last few days. I think I've caught up on my own."

"Are you sure? It's no bother."

"I'm sure." She reached over, touched his arm. "Thanks."

Now he turned his keen dark eyes on her. "For everything?"

He remembered! She smiled. "What else?"

A sweet note to finish the evening. Nevertheless, walking toward her front door, alone, the sound of his car disappearing around the corner, she felt a little sad. She would have to remember to make sure Michael came to Alice's party next Saturday.

CHAPTER ELEVEN

A week later, riding to the party in the Jaguar with Bubba and Nick, Michael was still thinking of Jessica's good night, and feeling bad. A couple of hours alone with him and she decides she doesn't even want his help with her homework. Hell of an impression he must have made. Yet for a few happy minutes here and there, over dinner and standing in line for the tickets before the Sara-Russ blowup, he had actually believed she liked him. He'd caught her staring at him a couple of times, watching him, thinking, he had imagined, how far-out he just might be.

She had probably been wondering when the night would be over.

Since then he had spoken to Jessica only in passing. He had taken to timing his trips to their locker so he would avoid her. He did so not because he was angry with her, but because he didn't want to bother her. She was so sweet; she might feel obligated to be nice to him even if she didn't feel like it. And he had another reason. She'd been spending a lot of time with Bill Skater the past week, at lunch and during break.

Beyond their mutual great looks, Michael couldn't imagine what those two had in common. Of course, from their point of view, that was probably more than enough.

"You're awfully quiet back there, Mike," Bubba said, driving. Nick sat to his right in the passenger seat. After dropping Sara and Jessica off the last Saturday, Michael had gone straight home. He had, however, seen Nick the next day at work and heard how well things had gone with Maria. But he had not spoken to Bubba about the *Big Night,* about Clair or Jessica. After all these years, Bubba usually knew when to leave him alone. Then again, it was Bubba who was dragging him to this party. If it hadn't been for him, and a fear of offending Alice, he would be at home now reading a book.

"That happens to me when I don't talk. You make a left here, in case you didn't know."

Bubba took one look down the road and drove past it without turning. Michael quickly saw his reason. The street was jammed, with cars everywhere. Though a quarter of a mile away from Polly and Alice's house, he could clearly hear the rhythm of the music, the sound of people laughing and carrying on.

"Your babe's going to be here, isn't she?" Bubba asked Nick.

"Yeah, Jessie invited her. And me, I guess."

"It doesn't look like they're turning away anyone," Michael said. Bubba couldn't find a spot anywhere.

"Is Clair coming?" Nick asked Bubba.

"Yeah. Wait till you see her in this new bikini I bought her. For all the material they used, it could have been cut from a red handkerchief."

"How did you keep her from exploding when she found out you weren't going to the concert?" Nick asked.

Bubba looked over at him. "Do you consider your-self a gentleman?"

"I suppose."

Bubba pointed to the glove compartment. "Open that, take the box out."

Nick did as he was told. Bubba was referring to the box of condoms he had been showing off last week. "There're only two left," Nick said, peering inside.

"That's why," Bubba said simply.

Michael snorted. "You didn't have sex with her eight times before ice cream and the movies."

"Four times before, three and a half times after," Bubba said.

"I don't believe it," Michael said. "I bet you didn't even kiss her good night."

"Maybe I didn't kiss her good night. I don't remem-ber. She fell asleep in my arms."

"That's B.S.," Michael said. "How could you get her in bed?"

"For the faithful romantic, no explanation is neces-sary. For the unbeliever, no explanation is possible."

"You probably got her loaded."

"I confess to offering her a couple of drinks."

"I bet she was unconscious the whole time," Mi-chael said. He didn't know whether to believe him or not. In either case, he realized he was jealous.

"What was the halftime like?" Nick asked, curious.

Bubba smiled. "And you said you were a gentle-man."

They ended up parking two blocks away. Climbing out of the car, Bubba donned a pair of sunglasses and a hat, even though the sun had set two hours earlier. He already had on a flowery Hawaiian shirt and a pair of brilliant red baggy swimming trunks. Nick offered to carry the case of Heineken Bubba had purchased—with the help of a phony I.D. Michael tucked his trunks in his towel, lagging behind his friends as they walked toward the huge, brightly lit house.

A number of people were gathered on the long steep front lawn. Michael thought he saw Dale Jensen, his main competitor for valedictorian honors, sucking on a joint. Neither of them let on he had seen the other.

Loud and crowded, the beautiful living room had changed from the last time he'd been there. Furniture had been cleared away from the center of the floor, a thick clear plastic laid down. The dancers could have used a referee. You couldn't even hear yourself talking.

Nick deposited the beer in an ice chest in the kitchen, then he and Michael followed Bubba down the hall to a relatively quiet game room. The main attractions here were a pool table and three separate video games. Michael searched for Jessica, hoping to find her so he could avoid her.

Russ had planted himself in the corner in front of the full-color graphics Demon Death. He had a joy stick, a full pitcher of beer, and Polly to help him back to safety from the realm of the dead. She was all over him. Sara mustn't be around.

On the other side of the room, on a low couch behind a table covered with snack bowls, sat Bill Skater, Clair Hilrey, and The Rock. The latter glanced up the instant Nick entered, leaned over, and whispered something to his quarterback. The team had lost the previous night: 17 to 7. Bill had thrown two interceptions and had spent the entire second half on the bench, when Tabb had scored its only touchdown. The Rock had played the whole game and had sacked the opposing quarterback four times. He was a strong SOB.

"Maria might be outside," Michael said to Nick.

"She might be in this room," Nick said. He had

gained a measure of self-confidence in the last two weeks.

"She's not in this room," Michael said. "And there's no sense looking for trouble."

"All right," Nick said, turning to leave. "But I can't keep avoiding him. You know that."

"We'll see."

Nick left. Apparently Bubba saw trouble, too. He didn't approach Clair right off the bat. He waited till Bill and The Rock were distracted, caught her eye, gesturing for her to meet him outside. Clair shook her head. She didn't mind hanging on to Bubba as long as no jocks were around. Yet Bubba persisted with his gestures, and finally she stood, excusing herself and silently passing within inches of Bubba as she left the room.

"There's a girl in love," Michael observed.

"Even the best of them suffer from guilt now and then," Bubba responded, not worried.

"Face it, she doesn't want to be seen with you when all her friends are around."

Bubba didn't appreciate the remark. "I didn't see Jessie running to welcome you with open arms at the door." He went after Clair.

"Sorry," Michael called after him. He was off to a great start. He noticed a Ping-Pong table set up in the garage off the game room. He often played against his mom at home; they were both good. He went and got in line for the next game.

He was a point away from being handed the paddle when he saw Jessica enter the game room and sit down beside Bill on the couch. They seemed happy to see each other. Bill handed her his drink. She offered him a pretzel. Michael accepted the paddle and crushed his opponent's initial serve into the table. They needed to get a fresh ball. He handed the paddle to the guy behind him and got out of line.

I could walk home. It would only take a couple of hours.

He once had read a discussion about which was the worse pain: severe emotional or severe physical pain. The article had come to no conclusions. Now he could see why. One always brought the other. He actually felt as if he had been knifed through the heart. He felt the urge to shout, to run away, but he didn't have a shred of energy to move. Most of all, he felt angry at himself for caring. What did he have to care about? They hadn't gone together. He had nothing to feel sad about losing. What he had was exactly that—nothing. Looking at her didn't even bring him pleasure anymore.

He would have left if Alice hadn't suddenly appeared at his side. He felt her before he saw her. She was hugging him. "Mikey, you're very, very late," she scolded.

He hugged her back. Touching her seemed to lessen his disappointment. "How come I hardly ever see you at school?" he asked.

She stood back a step. She looked thinner than he would have liked, but color had returned to her cheeks. Her clothes surprised him: plain blue jeans, an oversize green sweatshirt—and she had a closet of dresses to choose from. She read his mind, as she often did.

"I wore this for you," she said. "Don't you remember?"

He smiled. "When you came into the store at Christmas? Yeah, but you were ready to paint then."

"I'm going to paint tonight," she said, suddenly serious. "When everyone's gone." Then she smiled. "I'm happy you're here. I have to talk to you."

Bubba chose that moment to reappear, hat and dark glasses still in place. "Hello, Crackers," he said to Alice.

"Hi, Johnny," she replied in the same flat tone. Michael understood Alice's choice of greeting—John was Bubba's real name after all—but he had never heard the Crackers nickname before.

"Clair's changing," Bubba told him. "So are Nick and Maria. It's time for a little dip."

Alice warmed at the suggestion. "Yeah, Mike, let's go in the pool. Polly's been on me all night about playing the hostess, and I'm getting sick of it. I'll dump a half gallon of bubble bath in the filter. It'll be great! You dive off the board, and you don't know what you're going to land on."

"Isn't that dangerous?" Michael asked. He supposed he couldn't leave now.

"No, that's a great idea," Bubba said. "With the bubbles, we can all go skinny dipping." He glanced at Alice. "As long as that doesn't offend the kids?"

Alice didn't answer immediately, sizing him up. "Sara's here. She's upstairs, in case you didn't know."

"So?" Bubba said.

Alice slowly stepped around him, forcing Bubba to turn to follow her. "She didn't expect to be elected president," she said. "She was really surprised. Everyone was, except me. I know you used your computer to change the vote count."

It was Bubba's turn to size her up, his thoughts effectively hidden behind his dark glasses. Michael had of course suspected Bubba had altered the outcome of the election. After studying how the votes were collected, however, and the structure of the program used to count them, he had been unable to figure out how it could have been done. He had, therefore, not confronted Bubba with it. In reality, Michael couldn't have cared less who was school president.

"I didn't," Bubba said finally, his voice low and even. "And I don't care whether you believe that or not. But I do insist you stop accusing me of having access to confidential files, especially when other people are around. I told you on that first day—talk like that could get Mike and me expelled."

Alice laughed at his seriousness. "You're such a wonderful liar! I love it! Don't worry, Johnny, I'm not turning you in. Not tonight at least. Come on, let's go swimming. Let me go change."

As Alice left, Bubba looked at Michael and shook his head.

Polly was upset. She'd printed up sixty invitations and at least three times that number had barged through her front door. These people—they didn't care how much they ate, what they dropped on the floor. And they were so noisy! At Alice's insistence, she'd combined the speakers from their two bedroom stereos and arranged them in the corners of the living room. When the dial on the receiver was set at six, the house vibrated. Naturally, someone had jacked the setting up to ten! She already had a splitting headache. She almost hoped the police showed up when ten o'clock rolled around and neighborhood noise restrictions went into effect. It was going to take something drastic to get this herd out of here. She wished she had never allowed herself to be talked into this blasted party. That Alice—she got her way too much.

Polly had another reason to be angry at her sister. Despite her promise, Alice had invited Clark to the party.

"How do I kill these ugly critters here?" Russ

asked, nodding at the TV screen, slurring his words. He'd asked for a little whiskey in his beer. She didn't mind obliging him, though ordinarily she hated the smell of alcohol. She considered Russ a very special guy. He seemed to like her.

"You have to identify who they are first, what their powers might be. Most witches you can just shoot at and kill. But a disembodied spirit, you need a magic potion to get rid of them."

"Huh," Russ grunted, rubbing his red eyes. The poor dear, it had been hot again yesterday afternoon when he'd run the cross-country race. She'd been one of the few present, shouting her support. She'd been glad when he won. Sara and Jessica hadn't bothered to stop by. "What are these?" he asked.

"Witches," she said. "Just blow them away and go on."

He fumbled with the button on the joy stick. "They won't die," he complained. They wouldn't die because he kept missing them by several inches. Frustrated, he dropped the joy stick on the floor and took a gulp of his beer. She had never seen anybody, teenager or adult, who had his thirst. He belched loudly. "Where's Sara?"

She smiled pleasantly. "She not here. She's sick."

"Sick?"

"She gets sick a lot. I never get sick. I'm one of the healthiest people I know. At the hospital, they're always having me come back to donate blood."

Russ looked confused. "I've got to talk to Sara."

"Why? You can talk to me."

He tried to stand, without much success. "She's got my axe."

Polly put him back in his chair. She had just spotted Alice heading for the living room, possibly for upstairs. That girl had better not be planning to go in the pool. Someone had to keep up with all these guests. Polly felt she had already done more than her fair share.

"Stay here," she said, getting up. She still had the axe in the trunk of her Mercedes. "I'll try to find it for you."

Russ scratched his head. "Why did Sara give it to you?"

Leaving the game room, Polly noticed Jessica gossiping with Bill Skater. Clair Hilrey vanishes for a second and Jessica takes her place. The same thing had been going on all week at school. Polly thought Jessica a fool. She had a sharp guy like Michael Olson interested in her, and she pursued a lug like Bill. If she had a guy, Polly swore, any guy, who really respected her, she would treat him right. Jessica had a lot to learn.

Alice did indeed head upstairs. Polly followed her carefully. They'd placed a sign on the front door stating the top floor was off limits. A few people had ignored it, to use the second-floor bathrooms, which Polly supposed was better than their using the bushes.

Two short flights of stairs led to the upper floor. Polly paused on the landing. Alice was talking to that greasy guy from the gas station near the turn in the hall. *Kats*—another example of someone they had not invited. With the loud music, Polly couldn't hear what he was saying. But she didn't like how he was grinning at her sister. She wouldn't be surprised if Alice was encouraging him.

She changed her mind a moment later. Kats wouldn't let Alice into her room. He'd stretched his hairy arm across her bedroom door. Alice looked around uneasily. Polly hurried up the remaining flight of stairs, strode down the hallway.

"Hi," she said to Kats. "How are you?"

He took his hand off the door frame, stepped back. "Great! Far-out party you're having."

She smiled. "I'm glad you're enjoying yourself." She took Alice by the arm. "Excuse me, I have to speak with my sister."

She led Alice around the corner and into the room at the end of the hall. It used to be their parents' bedroom years ago. Polly opened the door, turned on the light. A sudden flash dazzled her eyes. The light died. Old bulb, burned out. She stumbled forward, searching for the lamp on the nightstand in the corner. They were the only two pieces of furniture in the room. There wasn't even a rug.

"What was that all about?" she asked, turning on the lamp.

"Nothing," Alice said, closing the door behind her. "He wanted to talk, and I wanted to get into my room and change."

The floor had recently been polished. The glare of the light from the lamp's naked bulb reflecting on the hard wood irritated Polly's eyes.

"You're not going in the pool."

Alice put her hand on her hip, pouted. "Yes, I am."

"That isn't fair. I'm sick and tired of running all over the house making sure everybody's having a good time. I'd like a few minutes to relax."

"Fine, relax. The party will carry on just fine without either of us."

"Sure, just drop everything. In case you didn't know, we're out of paper cups downstairs."

Although the room appeared empty, its closets were jammed. They kept Christmas decorations, party stuff, etcetera in the space where their parents had hung their clothes. Earlier, while preparing for the party, they had gone through the closets. There was still an aluminum ladder parked against the wall. Taking hold of the middle rungs, Alice spread it out beside one closet.

"I'll get the cups," she said. "Then I'm going in the water. I don't care what you say."

"Who'll greet the guests? Not me."

"Most of the guests are here. A lot of them are already leaving."

Polly moved closer, stepping in front of the lamp, casting a shadow over her sister. "Somebody is not here yet."

Alice paused halfway up the ladder. "He's not coming," she said.

"He said he was when he called this afternoon. That's what he told me." She took another step closer, put her hand out to support the ladder. It was old, unsteady. "Why did you tell him about the party?"

"I didn't."

"Then how did he find out about it?"

"I don't know."

"I don't believe you."

Alice closed her eyes briefly, leaning her head back, taking a deep breath. Her doctor had taught her that, just breathe and blow your troubles away. A bunch of hogwash. "I told you, I'm not seeing him anymore. I didn't tell him about the party. He must have heard about it from someone else. Jessica, or Sara maybe."

"Neither of them has even met Clark."

"He could have called when they were helping us get ready this morning. One of them could have answered the phone."

"Did they say that?"

Alice shook her head, went up another step. "Leave me alone."

"You want me to let go of the ladder? If I do, you'll fall and break your neck. Anyway, why are you suddenly down on Clark? What did he do?"

Alice opened the closet, pulled out a mass of tangled Christmas tree lights. "Nothing."

"Did he say something about me?"

"No. What would he say about you?"

"Oh, excuse me, I guess you've forgotten I used to go out with him."

Alice tried pushing the lights aside, trying to get to the brown box that held the paper cups. The Christmas lights kept tangling in her hands. "I know who told him about the party," she said softly.

"Who?"

"You."

Polly let go of the ladder, chuckled. "What?"

Alice glared at her. "Admit it, you wanted him to come tonight. I've broken up with him, and you want to see if you can get him back. Well, he's not coming. I called him not three hours ago and told him he wasn't welcome."

"Why, you little—"

"Listen to me, Polly! Stay away from him. He doesn't just have weird ideas, he does weird stuff. He's dangerous."

Polly found herself trembling. How dare her sister, her *baby* sister, talk to her this way! Such filthy lies! Yet she didn't yell at her. The top of a ladder was no place to fight. There could be an accident, somebody might get hurt. She knew about that sort of thing. She tried to calm herself.

Besides, she was—*curious*. "What sort of weird stuff?" she asked.

Shaking her head, Alice climbed down. "I'm going. Good-bye." She opened the door.

"What about the cups?" Polly cried.

"I'll get them later," Alice called over her shoulder, slamming the door behind her. Polly stood for a moment staring at the bright bulb, even though it hurt her eyes and made her headache worse. She hadn't invited Clark. Why would Alice say that? She was pretty sure she hadn't invited him. And she had a good memory for such things.

Polly resolved not to get the cups no matter who complained. Alice had said she would take care of it, and Alice had to learn to be responsible. But while the ladder was out, she figured she might as well change the overhead bulb. The lamp didn't go on when you threw the switch by the door. She didn't want someone looking for the bathroom stumbling and breaking a leg.

Polly found a package of 100-watt bulbs beside the Christmas lights. Holding the replacements in one hand, she scooted the ladder to the center of the room with the other. Climbing the ladder, she reached around the shade and began to fiddle with the old bulb. She couldn't see it but she could feel it, dusty and delicate beneath her damp fingers.

All of a sudden, she realized exactly how wet her hands were.

Russ must have spilled some beer on me or something.

The light switch beside the door remained in the on position. The bulb couldn't have been completely dead. As she turned it counterclockwise, it flickered on. Water and light bulbs make poor companions. It exploded in her hand, and her fingers slipped directly into the charged socket.

The electric shock shot through the length of Polly's body. Her footing vanished beneath her. She had no chance to brace herself for the fall. She hit the floor on her right hip, hard, the impact sending a jolt through her spine and into her skull. Her headache blossomed from a minor irritation into a red wave of agony.

Then everything turned dark and cool, for how long she wasn't sure. When she opened her eyes next, the ceiling looked miles away. She sat up, shook herself. The fingers of her right hand were bleeding. She slowly got to her feet, using the wall for support. Glass from the shattered bulb lay scattered across the hard wooden floor.

Lord, I could have electrocuted myself.

She needed a bandage for her hand. She could fix the bulb another time. Clark might show up any moment. She did remember now; she had told him to come over late, after most of the people were gone. That didn't excuse Alice's insolence, though, not by any means. She would have to have a word with her about being respectful, for her own good.

Bill Skater didn't talk much. Jessica had always been attracted to the strong, silent type. Like Michael, she had discovered Bill to be an excellent listener. She did wish, however, that he would occasionally volunteer something. Hanging out with him, she often felt as if she were playing bounce with a flat ball.

The Rock, on the other hand, enjoyed talking, and surprisingly, had much of interest to say. He was telling her about the work he did with disadvantaged kids downtown. He had a loud, boisterous voice, and a childish enthusiasm she found appealing. In many ways he was like one of the kids he helped. She and Bill were drinking beer, but The Rock had ten minutes ago recoiled from her offer of one as if she had suggested a deadly shot of heroin. He had quickly reassured her that he had nothing against her drinking, it just wasn't his style.

"We have it so easy in this part of town," The Rock said. "We have the ocean to swim in, the beach to run along. Everything's clean: the stores, the sidewalks.

But in the ghettos, those kids have nothing but asphalt, plugged sewers, and drugs. There're dealers everywhere. Crack's the big thing these days, that hard cocaine people smoke.'' He shook his head in disgust. ''Just last week I was approached by a twelve-year-old kid trying to sell me the stuff.''

''How did you get involved in the Big Brother Program?'' Jessica asked. He had such obvious sympathy for black kids, she wondered how the feud between him and Nick had ever started. She didn't have the nerve to ask.

''I had to pick up a pal at the L.A. bus station. You know where that is, right in the heart of the city? There was this black kid—found out later he was only eight—bumming change at the entrance. He hit me up for a nickel. Imagine, just a nickel! I asked him what he wanted it for. He told me food. I took ahold of his arm. It felt like a chicken bone.''

The Rock went on to describe how he took him for a sandwich and learned how the boy slept in a garbage dump. He discovered there were dozens of kids like him all over the city, that they had no parents, no one to help them. His conscience called. He became a Big Brother. To this day, he regularly saw that first boy— Emmanuel.

Then The Rock switched the topic to football, and almost immediately Jessica found her mind wandering, back to the previous Monday morning when Bill had approached her after Mr. Bark's political science class. That morning she'd had to read a paper on why she thought the electoral college system should be abolished. Mr. Bark had given her an A on the piece. She had spent three hours researching the paper in the library the previous day. Bill had wanted to compliment her on a job well done. Those were, in fact, his exact words. She had blushed.

"Thank you. But to tell you the truth, I didn't understand half of what I was saying."

"I thought you were very clear," he said. He had an unusually smooth complexion. The blue of his eyes reminded her of the Mediterranean skies of her vacation. "What was your name?"

"Jessie."

"That's right." They talked for a few minutes about purely inconsequential matters: the weather, the state of the union. Finally the question came. "What are you doing for lunch, Jessie?"

Life was good. Her legs felt weak. She told him she was free.

He took her for Chinese food in the mall. She had fun. Well, she had fun looking at him. They didn't exactly enjoy an instant rapport. Possibly because the team was doing badly, but he wouldn't even discuss football. She still didn't know what his interests were. Since Sara had told her how assertive he could be during student council meetings, she found his shyness confusing. Over lunch, and at other times in the week, he often seemed uncomfortable in her presence. She decided she would have to give it time. She had already made up her mind about one thing. She wanted to have sex with him.

A girl is always supposed to remember her first. Why shouldn't I start with the best?

Jessica was tired of daydreaming about making love. She had been doing that since she was in the seventh grade. It left her feeling unsatisfied, to say the least. It left her frustrated. She wanted the real thing, and she wasn't going to wait till she got married. It wasn't only because she was horny, she was just incredibly curious to see what it was like. When Bill finally asked her out on a real date, if he made a move, she had already decided she wasn't going to stop him. She couldn't wait to see the rest of that hard body. She was already investigating types of contraceptives.

Her decision surprised even her. A year earlier it would have been unimaginable. She had always considered herself fairly moral. For instance, her cheating on the chemistry quiz still bothered her. But her outlook had grown far more liberal in the last year, largely because of her European vacation. When she had first arrived on the beaches of southern France, and seen people nude sunbathing, it had been a shock. But by the end of the week—when her parents weren't around, of course—she had joined the crowd.

But there was still that big question—*when* Bill asked her out. When was that going to be? Clair had to be the reason for the delay. Jessica had never spoken to him when she was around. The one time she had broached the topic of his involvement with her, he had changed the subject.

The Rock wrapped up a story about some opposing lineman whose knee he had cracked in a dozen places and went off to change into his swimming trunks. Left alone with Bill, Jessica racked her brain for something to talk about. Bill continued to sip his beer, watching things go on about him. Suddenly Clair swept back into the room in an unfastened beach coverup and red bikini. In a cheerleader uniform, Clair projected a certain sex appeal. In this reasonable excuse for total nudity, she looked positively nasty. All legs, chest— enough clear brown flesh to exhaust any red-blooded American boy's fantasy reserve. Bill started to stand up. Clair grabbed his hands and pulled him into her arms.

"Let's go big boy," she said. "Time to get wet." She glanced up. "Time to get down."

"All right, I'll be there in a minute."

Clair grinned and asked what on the surface appeared to be a redundant question. "In the pool?"

"Yeah," Bill said.

She patted his rump. "OK, OK, the water first. Hurry." And completely ignoring Jessica, she turned and left.

"Did you want to go swimming?" Bill asked uneasily, setting down his beer.

Why buy contraceptives when I might be able to borrow Clair's?

She had bought a new bathing suit for the party. To compete with Clair, however, she should have purchased breast implants. She smiled, although it hurt to do so. She wouldn't ask what the deal was, not yet. "Another time, maybe," she said.

Alone, she started to search for Michael. She'd seen him come in. She just wanted someone to talk to.

Summer had come to an end. Feeling the chill of the nighttime air as he huddled his shoulders beneath the warm water and fluffy bubbles, Michael felt autumn inside. He always mourned the summer's passing and instantly began waiting for it to return. Somehow, this year, he could tell, it was going to be a long wait. He continued to think of Jessica and Bill together on the couch.

"Marco!" Bubba called, paddling through a bank of foam in the deep end, his eyes tightly clenched, playing the blindman in the oldest pool game ever invented.

"Polo!" three dozen people replied. Marco Polo in a pool as crowded as this was a joke. You just had to launch yourself in practically any direction and you were bound to tag somebody. Naturally, Bubba had been *it* for the last twenty minutes. Michael suspected he was slyly opening his eyes so he could stay *it* until he could accidentally rip the top off a girl of his own choosing.

"Marco!"

Maria and Nick swam to Michael's side. "You two look like you're having fun," he said.

"The water feels great after working all day," Nick agreed.

"I think we should get out," Maria said, glancing toward the diving board where several of the football players had gathered to taunt Bubba into coming their way.

"You might," Michael said.

Nick shook his head. "I feel just fine where I am. Anyway, what can they do to me in front of all these people?"

"They could drown you," Maria said unhappily.

The boys on the team did not try to drown Nick. But they did pull a rather unpleasant stunt. Much to Bubba's obvious displeasure, he bumped into The Rock, and was no longer *it*. As the center of attention, The Rock, with supposedly closed eyes, wasted no time in heading straight for Nick, who made the mistake of moving away from the side of the pool. Several guys on the team suddenly popped to the surface behind Nick. He saw them at the same time Michael did. It did neither of them any good. One grabbed Nick's right arm, the other his left. His head got pushed under and The Rock went diving.

They all reappeared a few seconds later, with Nick thrashing wildly and The Rock laughing heartily. The Rock had torn off Nick's trunks.

"Come get me, boy," he taunted, moving into the shallow end where Nick would have to stay low—*real* low—if he didn't want to be the talk of the school on Monday. Yet Michael felt more afraid for The Rock than he did for his friend. The guys who had pinned

Nick's arms seemed to have reassessed Nick's strength in the short time they'd had ahold of him. They backed off, gingerly rubbing their sides, as the other guys on the team watched from a respectful distance. For the moment Nick had The Rock to himself, and Michael could not have imagined such fury in Nick's face. It was out of a similar expression the many ugly rumors concerning his deadly rage must have sprung.

But Nick couldn't move, except on his knees. Bubba clearly recognized the problem, and Bubba loved to watch a good fight.

"Hey, Nick!" he called from the deep end, his hands out of sight beneath the water and bubbles. "Take these!"

He didn't toss him a sword or a knife. Bubba threw Nick a pair of trunks—*his* own shorts. Nick caught them, put them on. The Rock backed into the side of the shallow end, stopped his taunting. Nowhere to go.

"Hey," he said.

Nick launched himself at The Rock, who had decided a fraction of a second too late that the water was not a safe place to be. Nick caught The Rock by the right arm and the back of the neck just as The Rock put one foot on the deck. The Rock started a cry that ended in a strangled gargle. Nick had shoved him under. The festive atmosphere hushed into a tense silence. It was a struggle for Nick—The Rock's feet and hands kept thrashing to the surface—but it was clear he could hold his prey's head under as long as he pleased.

"Stop!" Maria cried.

"No," Nick said.

"You'll kill him!" she pleaded.

"Yeah!" Bubba cheered.

Nick smiled grimly, tightening his grip. "Not yet."

171

Maria dived toward Nick and pounded him on the back. "Let him go now!"

Nick looked at her strangely for a moment. Then he held his hands up, as if he were displaying his innocence. The Rock broke the surface, his choking gasps material for pity. He lay bent over the steps, sobbing in recovery.

"We can't do this," Maria said wearily. She could have been talking about more than The Rock's dunking.

"He started it," Nick protested.

Maria shook her head sadly. To her, it didn't matter.

Michael watched the next few minutes with a calm fascination. To a casual spectator, the hostilities appeared to be over. The usual chatter resumed across the pool. Yet Michael knew they had merely passed into the eye of the hurricane. Worried about Maria's feeling, Nick paid little heed to the movement of people around him. The Rock was making a swift recovery. He had moved from the steps and now was sitting on the side near the diving board. One by one, his teammates, including Bill Skater, swam to his dangling feet, conferring with him.

"Nick," Michael said. "Nick."

His friend didn't hear, preoccupied as he was with convincing Maria that he hadn't intended to drown the fat slob. Perhaps it didn't matter, Michael thought. Help was on the way. Seconds before The Rock jumped Nick, Alice had been testing the pool's chlorine level. When they had a lot of people in the water, Alice had said, the level could drop rapidly. When The Rock had attacked Nick, Alice had dashed into the house, the pail of powdered chlorine in her hand. Now she reappeared with her sister holding the chlorine, just as The Rock reentered the water with eleven backups—and began to swim toward Nick.

"Nick!" Michael shouted.

He said violence follows him, no matter where he goes. In the streets, the weight room, the store, the pool . . . Could he be right?

It didn't take long for a person, or a dozen for that matter, to swim the length of the pool. It took Polly about the same interval to stride from her back door to the steps of the pool. When Nick finally did look up, he found himself surrounded by friends and foes alike.

"Get out of the water, all of you," Polly said.

"Sure," The Rock said, a purple welt swelling beneath his left eye. "After we take care of business."

Nick flexed his shoulders, the water reaching to his waist, shooing a terrified Maria aside. "Don't keep me waiting," he said to The Rock.

"My man!" Bubba shouted, off in the corner with Clair. He would be pulling off the bottom of her red bikini next and offering it to Bill. Tabb's quarterback, another upstanding member of the lynch gang, waited expressionless by The Rock's side. Michael edged toward Nick. If he had to fight to save his pal, he decided it wouldn't be bad to get in a stiff kick to Bill's crotch.

After all, the guy stole my girl.

What a laugh. He would probably get his head smashed in, and yet, he was pleasantly surprised to discover he wasn't afraid.

"You better pray you were born with gills, boy," The Rock said, glancing around to assure himself of his support. Nick did not move, but Michael could literally see the dark strength coiling in his muscles.

"No!" Maria cried.

"Get off my property!" Polly shouted at The Rock, jumping onto the first step, the water drenching the bottom of her black pants. She stuck a hand into the pail of chlorine. "Get!"

"Bug off," The Rock said, raising his fist, intent on Nick.

Polly threw a handful of chlorine in his face. Unfortunately for The Rock, he was soaked. The white powder dissolved instantly. The Rock let out a scream, his hands flying to his eyes. Michael grimaced. Chlorine solution could eat out eyes in seconds.

"Put your head under the water!" Michael said. "Get his head under!"

Bill tried to do just that. The Rock jabbed an elbow into Bill's jaw. *Don't you touch me*. Understandably, The Rock was not crazy about having someone submerge him again. He just kept screaming.

"My eyes! My eyes!"

Michael dived forward, grabbed The Rock's wrists. "Go under water—now—and blink your eyes or go blind!" he yelled in his ear. The Rock nodded once, thrust his head beneath the surface. He came up a few seconds later.

"My eyes!"

"More," Michael ordered, pushing him down. "Stay under a whole minute. Flush them out."

While he was submerged this time, Polly muttered something under her breath, dropped the pail on the ground, and strode back into the house. The others waited quietly. Alice entered the water to stand beside Michael. Finally The Rock reappeared.

"How are they?" Michael asked. "Let me see."

"They sting. They hurt."

And they were a nasty red. "But you can see," Michael said. "Go inside, into the bathroom, and take a shower. Let the cold water run straight into them for a few minutes, but not too hard. Keep your hands away from them. Then get dressed and have someone drive you to the hospital." Michael patted him on the back. "Go ahead, you're going to be all right."

The Rock did not look at Nick as he left. Maybe it hurt too much. The boys on the team dispersed. It seemed to be over, for the time being.

The night deepened. The suds began to vanish. In groups of twos and threes, people got out of the water. Bubba finally gave up his carousing with Clair and consented to wear a towel on the walk to the house. And Nick and Maria were long gone when Michael began to slowly swim laps, on his back, staring at the black sky, wondering if Jessica was inside with Bill hearing about how the tall black dude had tried to kill The Rock for a second time.

Michael was alone with Alice and she was flying through space, like an acrobat, maybe an angel, in her white bathing suit and shining yellow hair, performing dive after dive.

"Watch this one!" she called, jumping onto the board again.

Michael rolled onto his side. Lithe but coordinated, Alice stepped forward, pounced the board's tip, soared upward, gracefully spinning through two and a half somersaults. She disappeared head-first into the water with the faintest splash. Michael waited for her to resurface, ready to applaud her effort. *One . . . two . . . three . . .* Time passed so slowly when someone went under and didn't come up.

"Alice?" he said.

"Eeeh!" She laughed, popping up behind him, throwing her arms around his neck. "Scared you?"

"Yeah, fish brain." He grabbed her and threw her over his head as if she were made of air.

They got out awhile later. From the positions of the stars, Michael knew it must be near midnight. The music continued inside but at a lower volume. No one seemed to be dancing. He could hear few people talking. Handing him a towel, Alice led him around the side of the house to the spot where she had been painting last week. They'd set up a couple of barbecues earlier that needed extinguishing, she explained.

"Do you think Polly damaged that boy's eyes?" she asked, slowly raking the smoldering coals with a black metal stick. She didn't have what most people would call striking features, but at that moment, the burning orange light warm on her young face, she was, to Michael, a child of beauty.

"No. Very little of the chlorine got in his eyes. He's a baby, cries a lot. Don't worry, he'll be fine."

Alice smiled, not like an angel really, more like a mischievous devil. "I told you I wanted to talk to you. Do you know what about?"

"What?"

"Jessie."

"Oh?"

Alice stopped, watching him over the heat radiating from the flaked charcoal. The front of his body was burning, but goose flesh was forming on his back from a breeze that had begun to blow out of the east. He hugged his towel tighter. The tall silhouette of a two-armed cactus stood behind Alice in the garden like a prickly ghost.

"You knew she was the one I told you about," she said.

"Not at first. Not until the football game."

"Why didn't you tell me, after that?"

There was no accusation in her voice, simply curiosity. "Why didn't you tell her when you found out we were going out?" he said.

Alice nodded, as if to say "well answered." "Neither of us told her. What a coincidence. Or do you think the decision passed unspoken between us?'' Before he could respond, she continued, ''Yeah, I think so. But I was still disappointed I didn't get to introduce you two, that you found each other without me.''

''Why?''

Alice returned to scattering the ashes. ''Jessie's always taken care of me. When my parents died, and Polly was in the hospital, she became like another sister to me. No, more like a new mom. I don't think I would have survived without her. And then, when I met you at Christmas, I felt like I had found— Does this sound corny?''

''Not at all, Alice.''

She smiled shyly. ''I love you, Michael. You know that. You've always been like the other half for me. Jessie and you— I had this dream for a long time. I was saving each of you for the other, for the right time. Then when our schools got put together, I knew that time had come. Do you understand what I mean? Maybe it was selfish, but I thought that you would come together through me, and then—then it would be beautiful.'' Alice stopped. ''You love her, don't you?''

''I hardly know her.''

''But you still love her. I can see that. Don't worry, no one else can. I knew you'd love her.'' She lowered her head, suddenly frowned. ''I hope everything will be all right.''

He chuckled. ''Everything's going to be fine. Why wouldn't it be?'' He was glad she had not asked him to verify the truth of her statement. Her certainty, her insight, intrigued him, frightened him. She didn't even care how their date had gone. It was immaterial to her, or rather, it was simply material, and she was talking about something bordering on a spiritual bond. She stood on an edge where she could see in directions others couldn't. He'd known that from their first meeting, and it had drawn him to her. But how fine an edge? He worried for her.

"Because I wasn't there," she said, vaguely confused. "And in my dream, I was always there."

"When Jessie and I met?"

"Yes." She shook herself. "I probably dream too much. That's what my doctor says." She glanced up to the dimly lit second-story window above them. "That used to be my parents' bedroom. Polly cleaned it out a few years ago. Gave away all the furniture."

"You must miss them a lot."

She laughed suddenly. "That's what I'm trying to tell you. I don't! When I'm awake, I have you two wonderful friends, and then, when I sleep, I walk in the forest with my mom and dad. I honestly do." A spark flared between them, distracting her. She wrinkled her nose at the black and burning cinders. "This is something Clark would paint. Looks like hell. But then, he's a weird guy." She set aside her stick and slowly moved her hand inches above the center of the barbecue.

"Careful, you'll burn yourself."

"I'm wet, I can't get hurt."

He had doubts about that. He wished she would stop. Who was this doctor she had mentioned? "Tell me about your dreams?"

She nodded at his question. "I bet you dream, too."

"I do."

"I knew it. I'll have to show mine. We can compare them. I'm going to finish my painting tonight."

"Tonight? You should go to bed."

She took her hand back. If she had burned it, she would never show it. He pushed aside his concern. She was sensitive—true, but also strong. "I'm not

178

tired," she said. She glanced up at the window again. "I'd better go in. This charcoal can burn itself out. I just remembered, I promised Polly I'd get out some paper cups."

"But practically everyone's left."

She stepped around the barbecue, took his hand in her warm one, and led him toward the back door. "With Polly, it doesn't matter." She laughed. "Let's finish our talk later."

All in all, Nick thought, it had been an eventful evening. He'd had an invigorating swim, been in a messy fight, and had received the first kiss of his life from a girl only a few minutes after he believed he had lost her forever. Sitting on the couch in the living room with Maria and Michael, listening to a Beatle album on the stereo, he was glad things had finally slowed down. He didn't wish to disturb his present feeling of contentment—it had cost him too much to achieve.

"It's lucky my parents think I'm asleep in bed at Jessie's house right now," Maria said, nodding toward the polished brass clock on the wall as it struck one o'clock. "At home, I have to be in bed by ten."

"I haven't been in bed before ten since I was ten." Michael yawned, leaning back into the soft deep cushions. He'd dressed, but his hair was still wet from his swim. "I could go to sleep right here. Let's head out in a few minutes, Nick."

"We can leave now if you'd like."

"A few minutes. Where's Bubba?"

"I don't know." For the moment the three of them had the living room to themselves. They had, in fact, only the foggiest idea who was left in the house. Nick had seen Clair and Bill not long ago, heading up the stairs, and Kats wandering around the kitchen searching for a knife. That was it.

Even with the music on, the house *felt* oddly still. Despite Nick's feeling of peace and contentment the sensation was not pleasant. Late at night on the streets, in the worst parts of town, it often felt quiet like this.

"I'm glad I won't have to keep lying to my parents," Maria said. His reaction to The Rock's attack had terrified her as much as the attack itself. When they had gotten out of the pool, she wouldn't even talk to him. He'd feared that she thought he might one day go off the deep end and throw her around. But then, after she had changed into her clothes, her viewpoint shifted completely. The initial shock must have worn off. She told him how brave he had been. Then she had kissed him, briefly, but on the lips.

"What do you mean?" he asked.

"You're going to meet them," she said.

"Your parents? I thought that was out of the question?"

She wouldn't explain. "You're going to meet them," she repeated, leaning closer toward him.

Sara and Jessica entered the living room from the direction of the game room. Michael sat up suddenly. None of them had seen Sara all night. Maybe she had only recently arrived.

"Why is the music so loud?" Sara demanded.

"Someone must have turned it up," Jessica said. She sat in a chair at Michael's end of the couch. "I was beginning to think you were going to stay in that pool all night," she said.

Michael nodded. "I might have over done it. My eyes are sore from the chlorine."

"They can't be as bad as that jock's in the garage," Sara said, turning down the stereo volume. "That Polly had a lot of nerve."

"The Rock's here?" Michael asked, surprised. "Didn't he go to the hospital?"

"He came back," Jessica said.

Michael frowned. "Why?"

Jessica shrugged, looking tired. "Who knows?"

Wonderful, Nick thought.

Polly came into the room at that instant. Like Jessica, she seemed worn out, only more so. She wandered over to the record player. "I'm turning this off," she muttered. "My head hurts."

"Polly, where's Alice?" Michael asked.

Polly shook her head, trudged toward the back door. "I don't know where no one is." She pulled at the screen. "I've got to check on the chlorine level."

"Leave it until tomorrow," Jessica said.

Polly paid no attention to her, going outside, shutting both the screen and the thick sliding glass door behind her. Nick watched as she walked over to the water and picked up the small, blue chemical test box and pail of white powder she had used to stop The Rock. He had meant to thank her for coming to his rescue. Perhaps he'd do it when she returned—and when he came back from the bathroom. He had been scrupulously avoiding anything alcoholic. He didn't want Maria knowing he had any bad habits. But he had been putting away the soft drinks. His bladder was full. He got up.

"Where's the bathroom?" he asked.

"There's one off the game room," Sara said. "But I think someone's in there right now throwing up."

"Go upstairs," Jessica said. "Polly won't mind. There's one halfway down the hallway before you come to the turn. If that's being used, try one of the bathrooms in the bedrooms."

And so Nick started a walk he would for the remainder of the school year replay again and again in his mind, searching for a clue, for a reason for the horror that came upon them all at the end of Alice's party.

The stairway lay near the front door, close to the kitchen. Putting his foot on the first step, he heard a low moan off to his right. He paused, stretching his head around the tall potted plant that stood between him and the sound. It was Bill Skater, bent over the kitchen sink, his shirt rumpled, his face pale, as if he were about to be sick. Nick wondered if he should go to him, but then he remembered Bill beside The Rock in the pool. He continued on up the stairs.

He probably drank too much.

In the first stretch of the hall there were four doors, three on the left, one in the middle on the right. Jessica had specified the bathroom was in the middle, but had not said on which side. He didn't want to barge in on someone sleeping. He decided to skip the first door on the left, but tried the second door, finding it locked. He thought he heard water running inside. Chances were this was the bathroom Jessica had referred to. Yet he couldn't be sure. The sound could be coming from the last door on the left, or even from the one room on the right. It disturbed him that he couldn't narrow it down more specifically. The harder he listened, the more the faint gurgling seemed to spring from all around him. Of course that often happened with a faint noise in a quiet place. He could not hear the others downstairs.

He tried the lone door on the right. It opened easily, silently; a whiff of night air brushed his bare arms and face. The door led to an elevated porch that overlooked the pool. A dark figure stood alone at the edge of the square space, staring up at the sky, his booted foot resting on the roof's wooden shingles, which went right to the floor of the porch. A blue glow from the lighted waters below danced over his rough leather jacket.

Kats.

Nick closed the door carefully, confident the quirky gas station attendant didn't know he had been there. He moved to the third door on the left.

It was also locked, and had faint stirring going on within. Nick did not intend to be nosy, but he stood long enough and close enough to the door to pick up on the sounds of breathing, of shifting bedsprings. He heard a cough, a sigh, enough, he decided, to keep him from knocking. He walked on, making a right at the turn in the hall.

This part of the hallway presented him with a choice of two doors, both on the left. The first was locked. He almost knocked. There were people inside; he could hear them. What stopped him was a sound of soft groaning. He or she or they—Nick couldn't be sure—seemed to be in pain. Nick thought of Bill downstairs. He wondered if there was a connection. Guilt pricked his conscience. What if someone was hurt, or being hurt?

Yet he walked on. He did not belong in a house this big, with its plush furniture and high beamed ceilings. He was an outsider still, though for the moment things were going well, with his job and school, with Maria. He didn't want to mess up again. He didn't want to walk in on another fight.

Reasons. Excuses.

His guilt chased him into the final room at the end of the hall. Its door lay wide open, an invitation into a dark place.

Nick reached inside without actually stepping through the doorway, found the light switch turned up. He flicked it down, then up again. The darkness remained. He glanced back the way he had come, uncertain what to do. The last light in the hall was around the corner. At the moment it was of little help.

Come on, after what you've been through, you can't be afraid of the dark.

Yet that was precisely the source of his hesitation. He did not trust the dark. It robbed him of his keenest sense, his first line of defense, and if The Rock really had returned to the party, as Sara suggested, maybe he was waiting inside this room with God knew how many of his buddies, waiting eagerly to pay Nick back for a near drowning and a pair of burned eyes.

At the last moment Nick almost turned and walked away. The reason he didn't was purely physical. Testing every upstairs door had consumed time. Now he either had to get to a place to pee immediately or he was going to have to run outside and find a bush. The Rock was only a possibility—his discomfort, a certainty. He stepped into the room.

It appeared empty, although he couldn't be sure. The illumination through the open windows—they faced east, away from the pool—couldn't have been more meager. Yet the draft pouring in from the outside sent a chill through him. Polly and Alice must love the fresh air.

His eyes adjusted to the gloom. He noted the outline of another set of windows on the right wall, their shades down, and a second doorway off to the left, with a tiny room beyond. He felt his way forward. Inside the small room, his fingers found another light switch. Yet he chose to leave this one off. He had definitely reached a bathroom; he could see the outline of the sink and the toilet. If he put on the light he'd only startle his eyes, and then he'd have to exit into the dark room completely blind.

Nick moved inside, closed the door. He took care of business quickly, flushed the toilet, and reopened the door. He was still in the bedroom, heading for the hall, when he suddenly paused in midstride.

Tommy?

That ominous silence he had noticed downstairs struck him again, only stronger this time. His head felt strangely full. He wondered for a moment if he hadn't accidentally drunk something alcoholic after all, even though he knew his uneasiness had nothing to do with booze.

My blood brother.

A seed of fear began to form deep in his mind. The feeling of *heaviness*, inside and out, was not entirely new to him. He had experienced it once before, two years earlier. But that had been in the middle of the night in a dark alleyway after a gang fight that had bought his best friend a switchblade through the heart. Later, he had come to understand he must have gone into shock lifting Tommy's head with its blank and staring eyes off the ground, watching the lifeless blood form a dark pool on the dirty asphalt beneath them.

He had not thought of Tommy since he had moved to this new neighborhood. Why now? He did not know. He did not care. He just wanted to get out of the room, back to the others. The breeze coming in through the wide open windows was giving him the shakes.

Nick strode into and down the hallway. He didn't pause at any of the doors along the way.

He had reached the top of the stairs when the shot exploded in his ears.

No. Lord, please, no.

He froze, the bang resounding throughout the house. For several incomprehensible seconds, he did not move an inch. Then he bolted blindly down the stairs, colliding with Maria on the landing between the two flights, knocking her down. Picking her up, he noticed her eyes were as wide as saucers.

"What?" she gasped, trembling in his arms.

"A gunshot," he said.

She nodded tensely, her eyes going past him, back the way he had come. "Up there," she whispered.

"Stay here," he ordered, turning away from her. She grabbed his arm roughly.

"I'm coming, Nick."

At the sound of the gunshot, Michael did not jump up or let out a shout. Instead, he closed his eyes for a couple of seconds. He did not think of who had died, who it might be, only that someone had died. He knew it to be true with a certainty that went beyond reason. He felt *death* in the house. He felt sick.

When he did look up, Sara and Jessica were already on their feet, holding on to each other. A moment later the back sliding glass door flew open. Polly stood staring at the three of them for a second, her face as white and cold as fresh snow, then flashed by them toward the stairs. Yet Michael was the first to reach the top of the stairs. A gun that had fired once could fire twice. For a moment he tried to hold the girls back. He was wasting his time. They had to see, all of them, no matter how bad it was. They heard Nick's voice around the hall corner. In a tight fearful knot, they stumbled down the first hallway and turned right. Maria and Nick stood outside the last door on the left, peering in at the dark. Michael came up beside Nick, felt for the bedroom light switch.

"It doesn't work," Nick said.

"Is anyone in there?" Sara asked them.

"There's a lamp in the corner of the room," Jessica said. She stepped forward. "I'll turn it on."

Michael grabbed her arm, stopped her. "No, all of you, stay here. I'll get it."

The room was big. He could feel its size although he could not clearly see. He could feel a cold breeze in his face, the blood in his heart. It was cold, too, the blood, and it felt as if it cracked—like ice—when his foot bumped into a soft heap on the floor. A body, a dead body. Michael could smell the blood.

Nick moved up behind him. Nick's eyes were sharper in the dark than Michael's. He noticed the body on the floor before walking into it. He knelt down beside it as Michael was stepping over it.

It. Not her. It. A nothing.

Michael knew who it was before he turned on the light. Why did he turn on the light? Why did he know who it was? The bulb drenched his eyes with harsh whiteness. He closed them again, for a moment, and counted to himself as he had while waiting for Alice to come up from her dive into the pool. He noticed that there was no carpet in the room. They had carpet in the garage, but not here. Nothing soft to land on, like the water. He turned and faced the others.

Statues. Tragic sculptures. Four girls: Maria, Sara, Polly, and Jessica—they all looked the same. Kats came up behind them. He looked different. Somehow uglier than usual. He was moving, that was it. All wired up and jittery. Michael did not want to move. He did not want to look down. But he did.

Alice.

Lying flat on her back. Gun in her mouth. Her lips resting around the barrel. Nick took it out gently. Her lips closed, matching her closed eyes. She looked peaceful. Then a drop of blood appeared at the left corner of her mouth, trailed over the side of her face, plopping in her bright yellow hair. It was still wet, her hair. The drop of blood spread upward along the strand, trying, it seemed to Michael, to get back to her head, back inside.

There was something wrong.

Drop after drop began to trail out of the corner of her mouth. And each one splashed into her hair and spread upward, downward, wherever it found a path. Yet the hair at the back of her head was already soaked red. A thousand drops had already come and gone before they had entered the room. She lay in a pool of red. The reason was very simple.

She had a hole in the back of her head.

"She's dead," Nick said, looking up at him. The gun in his hand and the quiet anguish in his voice hurt Michael almost as much as the sight of the blood. He stepped around Alice and stood close to the girls. Out of the corner of his eye, he saw Polly faint, Sara catch her. The others appeared: Bill, Bubba, Clair, and The Rock—in that order. And he felt Jessica holding on to him, her face buried in his shoulder, the warmth of her tears seeping through his shirt.

"I hope everything will be all right."

Michael didn't know these people. He didn't care about these people. Suddenly he saw and felt nothing that had to do with any of them. There were only the stars that had shone above him while he had swum on his back in the pool, the surprise touch of Alice's wet arms that had wrapped around his neck when he had begun to fear for her well-being.

"I love you, Michael. You know that . . ."

The yellow hair, the red blood, the repose of her sweet face—they all blurred into one ghostly form and began to move upward toward the stars, faster and faster. He chased after her, as best he could, but her arms began to slip away. The spirit began to fade, to fail. The stars went out.

She had put on the veil of his dream. She was gone.

EPILOGUE

The funeral for fifteen-year-old Alice McCoy was held on the Thursday following her Saturday night party, at twelve o'clock in the afternoon. The McCoy family, though rich, was not large. And despite the many friends Alice had made during her short days on earth, few came to the funeral. People mourn easily the victim, the unfortunate, but seldom the suicide. A notice in the local paper had listed the cause of death as a self-inflicted gunshot wound to the head.

Standing beside the coffin above the open grave, a yellow rose in his hand, Michael looked around and counted, including the black-robed minister, only twenty-eight people.

There should be thousands.

He was in a tunnel. There was a dim glow up ahead, twilight behind, black enveloping walls all around. He had not slept since the party, nor had he been properly awake. Unfortunately, he wasn't in shock. He had been crying too much for that. But only when he was alone. That was how he wanted to be from now on, alone, always alone until the day he died.

He listened to the last words. Old written words—it didn't matter whether they were true or not, he thought, the lines about "life everlasting" and "the valley of the shadow of death." They were still just words. It was foolhardy to believe they could bring any real comfort. They brought him none. It was ridiculous they even had funerals. He was glad when everyone began to leave.

He sat down beside the coffin, near the mound of brown dirt that would cover it. Clouds came and went overhead, and with them, the sun. He couldn't decide whether it was hot or cold. One minute he was sweating, the next, shivering. He still had his flower in his hand. He tried planting it in the dirt but it kept falling over. He couldn't imagine he was never going to see her again.

Time passed, a long time. Someone finally came up behind him. He assumed it was a grave digger, come to shoo him away. You have to go, Bud, we have to stick her in the ground now. But whoever it was said nothing, and finally Michael turned around.

"Hi, Nick," he said. "Were you at the funeral?" He honestly didn't know.

When Nick had come into the store that first day, he had had trouble saying two words. Then he had gone out with a girl and stood off whole mobs. Now he seemed to be back where he had started. He bowed his head, mumbled his words.

"I'm sorry I was late. They just let me out of jail."

"Lieutenant Keller let you out?"

"Yeah."

"That jackass," Michael muttered. "He had no right holding you."

"I wasn't alone."

Michael nodded. The lieutenant had detained The Rock, Russ, and Kats. Michael had spoken to Keller last night on the phone. Kats was the only one he was holding, he said, and that was only because they had discovered a number of unregistered firearms back at the hole Kats called his apartment. Keller did not feel Kats was guilty of murder. "It was a suicide, Mike. None of those kids killed that girl. She put the gun in her mouth and pulled the trigger. Simple as that. Let it go."

Ass.

"I want to talk to you about a few things," Michael said. He hardly recognized the sound of his own voice. His vocal cords felt as if they had been scratched with sandpaper. "Could I see you down by the parking lot in a few minutes?"

"Sure." Nick glanced nervously at the coffin, with its shiny azure-colored paint and inlaid gold flowers. As far as boxes went, it was nice. But who wanted to be in a box. "I didn't bring any flowers," he said apologetically.

"It doesn't matter."

Nick swallowed. "I'll wait for you."

When Nick left, Michael knelt by the coffin, touching it. A final good-bye, that's what he wanted to say. He thought about it a minute, but nothing came. And he knew why. She wasn't here, in this dead body. She had left that night. He had seen her leave.

Nevertheless, he suddenly wrapped his arms around the box as if he were hugging a flesh-and-blood person. He couldn't help himself. He cried as though she had just died in his arms.

Nick was sitting on the curb, next to his bike, when Michael, calm and composed, finally descended from the rows of tombstones. Nick had bought the bike with his first—and last—paycheck from the store.

"I have some bad news for you," Michael said. "While you were in jail, you got fired. I told the bosses you had nothing to do with what happened. They didn't care." He shrugged. "If you'd like, I can quit in protest?"

"No, don't do that." Nick did not seem surprised, nor did he seem to care. "It's always been this way in the ghetto. Go in the slammer, lose it all. Everything."

"Maria?"

Nick nodded.

"She doesn't think you did it, for god's sake?"

Nick winced, turning away. His voice came out small and hurt. "I don't know. She won't talk to me."

"Well, to hell with her then." He went and sat beside Nick on the curb. He had a bad taste in his mouth. He hadn't eaten that morning. He could taste only his bitterness.

"Did you want to ask me something?" Nick said hesitantly.

"Yeah, who killed Alice?"

That surprised him. "I don't know."

Michael sighed. "I'm sorry. I know you don't know. And I'm sorry about Maria. And your job. But I'll speak to some people around town I have connections with. I'll find you another place to work."

Nick nodded, hunched over. "I'd appreciate that." He paused. "I'll tell you everything I know."

"OK."

Nick spoke as if he were repeating something he had repeated endlessly at the police station. "I got up to go to the bathroom. I saw Bill in the kitchen. He was by himself. He looked upset. I went upstairs. I passed the first door on the left. I didn't hear anybody inside. I tried the second door on the left, the bathroom. It was locked. I *thought* there was somebody inside. I heard water running. I tried the one door on the right, the door to the porch. Kats was standing out there, by himself."

"Did he see you?"

"No."

"Go on."

"I tried the third door on the left. It was locked. It sounded like someone was sleeping inside. At the police station, Russ said it was him."

"Yeah, he also said he slept right through the gunshot and all the commotion. I don't see how anybody could have done that." He would talk to Russ himself, to all of them. "Go on."

"I went around the turn in the hall. There were two doors on the left. The first one was locked. But there were people inside. One of them sounded like they were crying."

"Are you sure?"

"No. It sounded weird. I don't know what was going on in there."

"But there was definitely more than one person in the room?"

"I'm sorry, Mike, I couldn't swear to it."

"I understand."

"I went to the last door. It lay wide open. The light wouldn't work. I went inside, anyway, went to the bathroom, and then came back out. That was it. I was on my way back down, at the top of the stairs, when I heard the gunshot."

"You didn't see anyone in the room where Alice died, didn't hear anything?"

"No, but—"

"What?"

"There was something in that room." He stopped for a moment, thinking, then he shook his head. "I can't say."

"Please, Nick. What did you see?"

"Nothing."

193

"You must have seen something, heard something?"

"No, it— I was scared."

"Scared? Of what?"

He shook his head again, perspiration appearing on his forehead. "I don't know. Just something in that room scared me. It scared me bad."

Nick had grown up in a dangerous environment. He could have developed instincts to recognize a threat, even if it was invisible. "When you turned on the light in the bathroom, you didn't happen to notice anything behind you?"

"I didn't turn on the light. I could see enough without it."

"That's odd."

Nick was worried. "The police thought so, too. They kept asking me about that. But you know, Mike, I'm telling you what I told them. I'm telling you the truth."

"I believe you." He thought of how often Bubba used that same line to call people a liar. Bubba had a way with words. The police hadn't arrested him. "Could Alice have been in the room?"

"I didn't see her. The police think she could have been, waiting to, you know, waiting with the gun."

"Or they think she could have entered the room from the bedroom next to it, right after you started back down? From the bedroom where you thought you heard someone crying?"

Nick nodded. "They say that's probably what happened, that it was Alice I heard crying."

A wave of disgust engulfed Michael. "What did they say when you told them you thought you heard more than one person in that next to the last bedroom? That you had heard wrong?"

Nick was watching him uneasily. "Mike, they're not trying to hush anything up."

"No! But they're not working overtime, either. They're looking for the simplest explanation. And they think they've found it. Alice put a gun in her mouth and pulled the trigger. Neat. Clean. Fill out the paperwork and close the file."

Nick pressed his knees together, fidgeting. "Who do you think killed her?"

"Someone! Another person. That's all. Or maybe a couple of people." He buried his face in his hands, the tears too close. "She was my friend, Nick. She was full of love, full of life. I know she didn't pull that trigger. I know it."

Nick wisely didn't say anything, letting Michael be. Michael finally sat up. He could feel sorry for himself later. "Lieutenant Keller told me last night where everyone said they were at the time of the shooting. Let me go over it again with you and see if it's any different from what you got out of him." He held up his hand, counting off the points on his fingers. "Bill said he was in the kitchen, having a glass of water. The Rock said he was in the upstairs bathroom, taking a shower. Kats said he was standing on the porch, looking at the stars. Bubba said he was out front with Clair, talking about the stars." Michael clenched his fingers into a fist. "The stars. Kats couldn't even tell you what one looked like, and Bubba and Clair—" He shook his head in disgust. "Is that what Keller told you?"

"In the beginning, they separated us, got each person's story. They always do that. But this morning Keller told me exactly what you just said."

"Did he tell you about the gun and the bullet?"

Nick nodded. "The gun belonged to Kats. It was

the same one he pulled on us in the store. Kats admitted it was his."

"Right away? Before we identified it?"

"I don't think so."

"What about prints? Keller told me yours, Alice's, and Kats's were on the gun, but only Kats's were on the bullet shell."

"Same thing he told me. Mike, I honestly don't think Keller's holding back on us."

"I wonder. Did Kats have an excuse for how his gun got in Alice's—hand?"

"He said he had no idea. He had it in his car, in the glove compartment. He didn't say why he brought it to the party. He's one of those strange dudes, you know, always has to have his piece handy."

"If he was out on the second-story porch, how come he didn't get to the bedroom until after us?"

"I don't know. But he's in trouble. He didn't have a license for the gun. Keller hasn't released him yet, and won't until someone bails him out."

"That just breaks my heart." Even if he hadn't pulled the trigger, if it hadn't been for Kats's weird hobby Alice would probably still be alive. Michael stood. "Thanks for the information. Can I give you a ride anywhere? You bike will fit in my trunk, I think."

Nick got up, too. "No. Being cooped up these last few days—I feel like I need the exercise. What are you going to do now?"

"Go to Alice's house."

Nick was concerned for him. "Why?"

"To look around."

Nick glanced in the direction of Alice's coffin, resting alone on the hill. "She seemed like a real neat girl."

Michael coughed painfully. "I always thought so."

* * *

The McCoy residence, from the outside at least, had not changed: high roof, long driveway, steep front lawn—all that money and what difference did it make in the end?

The red sedan parked out front, however, was something new. Michael stopped his car beside it, got out warily. The front door opened before he could knock. The honorable Lieutenant Keller himself.

They'd met the night of the party. He was nothing to look at. Although a trim six feet two and less than forty years of age, he struck Michael as soft, someone on the physical road downhill. He didn't know how to dress. He favored plaids, but the squares on his sports coat were much too big. He had a bald spot he tried to hide by parting his hair low and combing the thin brown strands over it; it only made his head look lopsided. And he had that grayish skin so often seen on the movie sleaze ball. Michael disliked shaking his hand.

On the other hand, Michael realized, his appearance probably had nothing to do with the dislike. When Keller had arrived at the scene of the crime approximately half an hour after the shooting, he had failed to take charge. True, as Nick said, he did separate them and, along with his fellow officers, had taken down their accounts of the events. But Michael had watched him the whole time, and he never saw the sharp eye, the attention to detail he would expect from a good detective. Also, the lieutenant had appeared to decide right from the start what had happened. To Michael, that showed an unforgivable lack of professionalism.

Yet it would be unfair to discard his positive qualities. He had proven himself sensitive to the stress they were under. He had personally taken it upon himself to make sure Polly was immediately given over into the hands of a psychiatrist who specialized in the care of victims of emotional trauma. He was not a bad man.

He's just not Sherlock Holmes. Or his distant cousin.

They said hello and shook hands. He asked how the funeral had gone.

"Fine, I guess." Michael shrugged. "I haven't really been to a lot of funerals." He nodded at the yellow ribbon in Keller's hands. "What's that from?"

"The doorway to the bedroom. We'd placed it off limits until our investigation was complete."

Michael found the remark ironic. Polly's aunt was staying with a cousin, and Polly was sedated in the hospital. Off limits to whom? His bitterness refused to stay down. "So now you can go home early, I suppose?"

The lieutenant looked disappointed. "Everyone keeps telling me what a sharp kid you are, Mike. They say you could be a genius. Think about it for a minute, the whole situation. Then tell me what you'd like me to do. Go ahead, do it."

"I don't need a minute to know you shouldn't have told the papers it was a suicide. Why didn't you at least say she'd died from an accidental gunshot?"

Keller sighed. "Mike, she had the gun stuck right in her mouth. How could that be an accident?"

Michael wished he would stop calling him by his name. He was going out of his way to be personal when Michael felt like screaming obscenities in his face.

"Right, you felt morally obligated to be a hundred percent honest and to ruin Alice's reputation. But never mind that, your question's a good one. How could it be an accident?"

The lieutenant shook his head. "We went over this last night. The facts have not changed since then."

"I'd like to ask you about a few of those facts."

Keller glanced at his watch. "I have to be at the station in a few minutes. I really don't have the time."

Michael chuckled without mirth. "But you said it yourself, I could be a genius. I might spot something you missed. Or is that impossible, that you might have missed something?"

"Are you always this rude?"

"I must be in a bad mood."

The lieutenant took a weary breath, looked past him over the lawn, northwest, in the direction of Jessica's house. Michael had seen Jessica at the funeral. She'd worn a black dress. It wasn't her color. Although he remembered her saying hello, he was unsure if he had answered her. For reasons unclear to himself, he hadn't even wanted to stand near her.

"You're talking about a locked-room murder, you know that," Keller said. "The screens on the windows in that bedroom were screwed down. Our best man went over them with a magnifying glass. No one's removed them in years. There's an opening to the attic in the bedroom closet, but there's a stack of boxes pressed against it. Those boxes, by the way, couldn't have been moved and replaced in five minutes, never mind five seconds. When you get down to it, there was only one entrance into that room. The door."

"And it was lying wide open. How can you call that a locked-room murder?"

Keller caught his eye. "Do you think Nick did it?"

"No."

"His prints were on the gun."

"Because he took the gun out—away from Alice."

"But if I was the murderer, I would have done the same thing. Touch the gun as quickly as possible so I'd have an excuse for having my prints all over it."

"Nick didn't do it."

"I don't think he did, either. But, from a purely technical point of view, he's the only one who could have."

"That's not true. When the gun went off, he had the entire hallway behind him, all those rooms at his back that someone could have ducked into."

"And how long did Nick take to get from the top of the stairway and back to the bedroom? Three seconds? Four seconds? He ran straight there, didn't he?"

Michael paused. He hadn't asked Nick that specific question. "I would assume."

"He did, he told me he did. And looking at him, I'd wager he can run pretty fast. Face it, Mike, there just wasn't time for anyone to enter the room with Alice, force a gun in her mouth, pull the trigger, and then hide in one of the other rooms."

Michael put his hand to his head. He couldn't think as clearly as he usually did. He needed sleep. "You're overlooking something. You believe Alice entered the room immediately after Nick exited, right?"

"Yes. Or she could have already been in there when he used the bathroom."

"But the first possibility, you feel that's the most probable?"

Keller nodded. "Chances are she was the one Nick heard crying in the next-to-the-last bedroom."

"Let's say she did enter the room right after he left. But let's also say she wasn't alone, that someone was with her, or that someone followed her. And let's imagine he, or she, killed her, but *didn't* leave the bedroom."

Keller frowned. "I don't know if I follow you?"

"The murderer didn't have to rush from the bedroom to hide in one of the other rooms. He could simply have stepped into the bathroom."

"Did you see anyone step *out* of the bathroom?"

"No. But Alice was lying on the floor, and the—Well, in the shape I was in, Kats or The Rock or Clair or Bubba could have slipped into our group without my knowing it. To tell you the truth, I don't know where any of them came from."

Keller thought for a minute. "They came in through the door," he said finally.

"Admit it, you never considered the possibility."

The lieutenant started to protest, stopped. "You are clever, Mike, like they said. All right, I didn't think of it. But I had a good reason. You had Maria, Jessica, Sara, Nick, Polly—part of the time—and yourself, and yet, not a single one of you said anything about someone coming out of the bathroom."

"*We* may have had a good reason. Perhaps the murderer didn't come out of the bathroom until we left the room. That's what we did, you know. None of us could stand to stay in there."

"And then, when you were all back downstairs, did this murderer calmly stroll out the front door in front of you all?"

"No. But he could have gone out onto the second-story porch, off the roof, and into the backyard."

"Are you ruling out those you've mentioned as possible suspects?" Keller asked.

"If the murderer joined our group without our seeing him, no. If he snuck off after we left, yes."

"How did he get ahold of Kats's gun?"

"He took it out of his car. Kats hasn't been able to lock that Mustang in years."

Keller thought some more. This time he ended up nodding. "There is merit in what you say. But it doesn't explain how he was able to get the gun into Alice's mouth and her fingers wrapped around the trigger?"

"That is a problem," Michael admitted.

"And what about a motive? If you don't have that, you've got nothing. Who would want to kill Alice? Who was this outsider?"

"Did anybody tell you about Clark?"

"No. Who's Clark?"

"He was Alice's boyfriend."

"Was he at the party?"

"I didn't see him."

"Then why bring him up?"

"I told you, he was Alice's boyfriend. You asked for a possible motive. He was a weird guy."

"What's his last name?"

"I don't know. I checked around and nobody knows. I even went to the hospital where Polly's being treated. I managed to get a note slipped in to her asking for his last name. She doesn't even know, and she used to go out with him."

"I find that hard to believe."

"He never told her."

"Wait a second, Polly used to go out with Alice's boyfriend?"

"Yeah. I met him once."

"And?"

"He had the strangest eyes."

"Who cares about his eyes. Did he seem capable of murder?"

"Yes."

"Do you know anything about him? Where he goes to school? Where he works?"

"No. All I know is that he's an artist, like Alice."

Keller took out a tiny notepad, jotted down a couple of notes. "How come I never heard about his guy earlier?"

"Clark is only a possibility. The others—they could have motives of their own."

"Such as?"

Michael shook his head. "Not right now. I need to think about it longer. But you could do me a favor. I want a look at the autopsy report."

"What for? She was killed by the bullet that came out of the gun. It's cut and dry."

"I'd still like to see it."

"I appreciate your desire to clear your friend's name. But you are only that, a friend. You're not family. I can't turn over that report to you without permission from Alice's aunt."

"If I get permission, will you give it to me?"

"What do you want it for? You're not going to discover something the coroner missed."

"I like to be thorough. What was the name of the coroner?"

"I'd have to look it up." He glanced at his watch again. "I really have to go now. If you want to talk more, Mike, call me at the station in a few days. Try to get me Clark's full name."

"I'll do my best."

Keller went to close the front door. "I don't have to tell you that what you've suggested is a long shot. From what Jessica Hart said, Alice sounded like a very unhappy girl."

Michael found every muscle in his body suddenly tense. When he tried to speak, he distinctly heard his jaw bone crack. "What did she say?" he whispered.

"How Alice still hadn't gotten over her parents' death. In fact, it was Jessica who gave me the name and number of Alice's psychiatrist." Keller consulted his notepad. "Dr. Kirby. I have a call into her, but she hasn't called me back."

"She wasn't seeing a psychiatrist," he said indignantly. "I knew her as well as anybody and she never said a word about—"

"I probably dream too much. That's what my doctor says."

He lowered his head. It changed nothing. Lots of people saw psychiatrists and didn't kill themselves. That goddamn Jessica, spreading such lies . . .

"Anything wrong?" Keller asked, peering at him.

"No."

"What were you saying about her psychiatrist?"

"Nothing. I'd—forgotten." He needed to change the subject, to get rid of this man. "Could you please leave the front door unlocked? I promise to lock it when I leave."

Keller trusted him. Giving Michael a fatherly pat on the shoulder, he got in his car and drove away.

Hope you have time to stop for doughnuts.

The instant he stepped inside the house, Michael felt slightly nauseated. More than anything, he wanted to turn around and leave. He walked up the stairs slowly, listening to his heart thumping against his rib cage. It was the only sound he could hear. He realized he was holding his breath, and had to make a conscious effort to let the air out of his lungs.

The bedroom door where Alice died was closed. Turning the knob, he half wished it was locked. But it wasn't, and the first thing he saw as the door swung open was the yellow chalk outline the police had drawn on the floor around Alice's body. He hadn't stopped to think how short she had been. He walked into the room and closed the door at his back.

There was another outline on the floor, at the top of the yellow chalk, rounder, darker; blood always left an awful stain. For a morbid moment, he wondered if any had seeped through the floor onto the aunt's bedroom ceiling.

The rest of the house was furnished exquisitely. This room, except for the lamp and nightstand in the corner, the shades above the windows, was empty. No paintings, ornaments, not even a photograph, hung on the featureless white walls. Alice had told him Polly had simply cleaned it out one day. Why? The parents were dead. The parents had slept here. Alice had died here. Curious symmetry . . .

The police had drawn a small circle of chalk beneath the east-facing windows. A black dot pinpointed the center. Michael knelt beside it. This was where the bullet had gone after it had exited the back of Alice's head.

He peered into the shallow hole. It appeared to go straight into the wall, parallel to the floor. He sat beside it and faced in the direction of the door. The hole was about level with his Adam's apple.

Was she sitting when she died?

The possibility filled him with disquiet. If a murderer had been holding her, it would have been easier for him to do so with her standing up. It would give the others another reason to think she had killed herself.

He noticed an aluminum ladder resting against the wall beside the bathroom. He figured the police had brought it in to assist in studying the room until he vaguely recalled having seen it when they had discovered the body. Why had Alice or Polly brought a ladder into the room? To get down the paper cups?

He went through the room systematically, verifying Keller's points: heavy closet boxes blocked the attic entrance; dusty screen screws that didn't appear to have been touched in ages. Nothing he found proved or disproved either of the hypotheses he had presented Keller. But there were two things he noticed that struck him as unusual.

First there were the tangled Christmas tree lights hanging from the top shelf of the closet. The police had not pulled them out; he definitely recalled seeing them the night of the party. He wasn't quite sure why he considered it significant. The overhead light had been shorted out. Wires were often used to short out other wires. The connection seemed tenuous at best.

The second thing was not even properly in the bedroom. Peering out the east-facing windows at the overhang of the roof, he noticed that a small portion of a nearby wooden roof shingle—at the very edge of the overhang—was broken off. Indeed, it looked as though someone had broken it off with the heel of a foot.

Did someone enter or exit the room over the roof?

It made no sense. With the screwed-down screens, any approach from the outside was impossible. And yet, when he searched both ways along the roof edge, he saw not a single other damaged shingle. Only this one directly outside the east windows.

He examined the bathroom, found the same immovable screens on the window.

He was leaving the bedroom when he noticed the fine glass shards in the center of the wooden floor. A quick examination revealed them to be from a light bulb. He grabbed the ladder, spread it in the middle of the floor. Going up the steps, he reached up and unscrewed the overhead light shade. A minute later he was staring at a busted light bulb.

But what does it mean?

Probably nothing. That was what he was afraid of.

He went through the remainder of the rooms on the upper floor. When he was done, he sat down at the top of the stairs with a paper, ruler, and pencil he had taken from one of the rooms and drew himself a diagram. He sketched the entire second floor, but only that portion of the bottom floor that seemed pertinent.

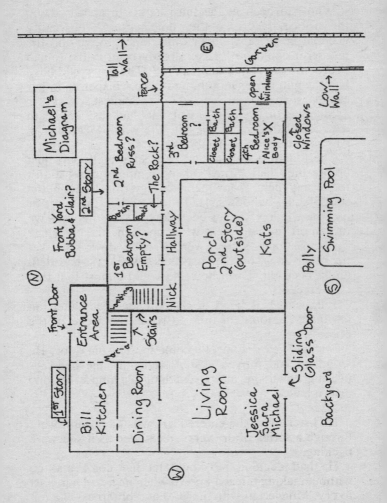

Michael's Diagram

1st Story

N

Front Door

Bill
Kitchen

Dining Room

Living Room

Jessica
Sara
Michael

W

Entrance Area

Maria

Stairs

railing

Nick

Sliding Glass Door

Backyard

Front Yard
Bubba & Clair?

2nd Story

1st Bedroom
Empty?

2nd Bedroom
Russ?

Bath

Bath

The Rock?

Hallway

Porch
2nd Story
(outside)

Kats

3rd Bedroom
?

Closet

Closet

Bath

Bath

4th Bedroom
Alice's X Body

open
windows

closed windows

Swimming Pool

Billy

S

Tall Wall

Fence

Garden

E

Low Wall

Who had been in the third bedroom appeared, on the surface, the crux of the whole matter. Yet in reality it could be of only minor importance. Alice and the murderer could both have already been in the fourth bedroom when Nick had entered. The guy could have had the gun in her mouth, and been whispering in her ear that if she so much as let out the tiniest sound . . .

Standing on the porch, Kats had had easy access to the roof of the house. Despite the window screens, it was something to think about.

The fourth bedroom had been extremely dark just before they had turned on the lamp. Michael didn't recall any light from the pool entering through the south-facing windows. Had the pool light been off or had the window shades been down? Would Polly have turned off the pool light while checking the chlorine? Those particular shades were certainly down now. Yet the other ones, on the east-facing windows, had definitely been up. Even now, he could almost feel that cold breeze.

Bill, who had been in the kitchen, had taken an inordinate amount of time to reach the scene of the crime.

Michael heard someone come in the front door. He stood up and moved a step back into the hallway, peering down the stairs, catching a glimpse of long brown hair.

Jessica.

He listened as she entered a downstairs room, went through a series of drawers. It sounded as if she were packing.

He had decided he would let her come and go without making himself known when he heard her start to cry. Mingled in with his grief and bitterness, he felt another emotion—guilt. Putting his diagram in his back pocket, he walked down the stairs.

She was standing in Alice's studio, her back to the door, touching a painting on an easel. She did not jump when he said hello. She merely turned, watched him through strands of hanging hair with those big brown eyes that had always worked such strange magic on him. They were red now, and puffy. She still had on her black dress.

"I saw your car out front," she said.

"Why didn't you call for me?"

"I knew you didn't want to talk to me."

He shrugged. "I'm here. We're both here. Why shouldn't we talk?"

She closed her eyes, sucked in a breath, her hands trembling. His tone had not been kind. She turned away. "I came to pick up some clothes for Polly," she said. "I'll be gone in a minute."

"Take your time."

Her back to him, her head fell to her chest. His guilt sharpened, yet so did his anger. "Michael, I don't understand," she pleaded.

The studio was the smallest room in the house. The numerous paintings and sketches were piled one on top of the other. Alice had had a dozen brushes and color trays going at the same time. She hadn't been what anyone would have called neat.

Michael had seen much of the work before. She used to bring her pictures into the store as she finished them: forest animals building a shopping mall in the middle of redwoods; high schools populated with penguin students—bright and silly situations that he had thought made up the best of her private universe.

As his eyes wandered over the room, however, he noticed a row of strikingly different works. A few were of alien worlds: a purple multitentacled creature feeding its hungry babies pieces of an American spacecraft; a hideous shivering skeleton trapped on an ice planet, trying to light a last match on the inside of its naked eye socket.

Before Clark. After Clark. I'll find that bastard.

Michael came farther into the studio, feeling in no hurry to answer Jessica's question. There was no carpet in here, either; and this floor was also stained.

"*I* don't understand," he said finally, leaning against the wall. "Here Alice gets murdered and the first thing her best friend does is tell the cops she killed herself."

Jessica stared at him, shocked, as if he'd slapped her across the face. Then her face collapsed in despair. A tear rolled over her cheek. Then another one. He held her gaze for a long moment, feeling his bitterness beginning to teeter as she began to tremble again. He turned away. This was bad. He had to stop. He wished he could stop. He just hurt so bad—it was as if pain had taken on a demonic character inside him and was demanding he make everyone suffer as he was suffering. But he didn't really hate Jessica.

I should have been there, in that room.

He hated himself.

It should have been me.

For being alive.

"I loved Alice," Jessica said, struggling with each word. "I loved her more than the world. And what I said to the police, I didn't say because I wanted to. It hurt me to say it, as much as it's hurting me now to stand here and have you accuse me of—"

She broke down then, completely, the sobs racking her body like shocks of electric current. He tried as hard as he could to go to her, to comfort her. Yet the insecure ego inside that he had deftly kept hidden all his adolescent years wouldn't let him. He was too afraid if he so much as touched her, he would break down, too. And that he could never do, not in front of her.

He stepped instead to the easel and pulled away the covering cloth.

Go forward, I will follow.

There was no desert, no bridge over a running river. Yet the lush forest and shimmering lake of Alice's final painting strongly reminded him of his dream. The colors were similar, and more important, the painting embodied the *feel* of his place.

He didn't quite know what to think. A lot of people, he supposed, dreamed of a Garden of Eden. That Alice and he shared similar tastes in paradise probably meant nothing.

Nevertheless, the painting somehow evoked the peace he'd experienced in his dream. A faint ray of that peace pierced his heavy pain. He reached out and touched the canvas. Alice had placed the two of them together, walking hand in hand along the grassy path that circled the edge of the clear water. She'd had only to complete the details of his clothing and she would have been done.

Then he noticed something else, a photograph of himself propped up beside the easel. He picked it up, as Jessica began to quiet down.

"I took it the night of the game." Jessica sniffed. "After you helped me with my camera, when you were sitting at the end of the bleachers with Nick. When Alice saw it, she told me she had to have it." Wiping at her eyes with her arm, Jessica gently plucked it from his fingers. She smiled suddenly. "I sort of wanted it for myself, but Alice asked, and she was all excited and—what the heck, I thought."

"Jessie."

"No." She set the picture on the easel at the base of the painting, picked up a small suitcase at her feet.

"Let's not talk, not now. I'll leave. I'll talk to you later. I'll see you at school."

He nodded. "Good-bye."

She turned away. "Good-bye."

To Be Continued . . .

Final Friends II:
The Dance

The party took one victim.
The dance would take another. . . .

Final Friends III:
The Graduation

The truth is finally revealed.
At a terrible price . . .

About the Author

CHRISTOPHER PIKE was born in Brooklyn, New York, but grew up in Los Angeles, where he lives to this day. Prior to becoming a writer, he worked in a factory, painted houses, and programmed computers. His hobbies include astronomy, meditating, running, playing with his nieces and nephews, and making sure his books are prominently displayed in local bookstores. He is the author of *Last Act, Spellbound, Gimme a Kiss, Remember Me, Scavenger Hunt, Final Friends* 1, 2, and 3, and *Fall into Darkness,* all available from Pocket Books. *Slumber Party, Weekend, Chain Letter, The Tachyon Web,* and *Sati*—an adult novel about a very unusual lady—are also by Mr. Pike.

AN EXCITING
NEW TRILOGY FROM

Christopher Pike

FINAL FRIENDS

No one does it better than Christopher Pike.
Master of suspense, Christopher Pike sets
the scene for mystery, intrigue and romance
in his new whodunit trilogy FINAL FRIENDS.

☐ *#1 THE PARTY* 73678/$3.50

☐ *#2 THE DANCE* 73679/$3.50

☐ *#3 THE GRADUATION* 70012/$2.95

From Archway Paperbacks

Simon & Schuster, Mail Order Dept. FFF
200 Old Tappan Rd., Old Tappan, N.J. 07675

Please send me the books I have checked above. I am enclosing $_____ (please add 75¢ to cover
postage and handling for each order. Please add appropriate sales tax). Send check or money order—no
cash or C.O.D.'s please. Allow up to six weeks for delivery. For purchases over $10.00 you may use
VISA: card number, expiration date and customer signature must be included.

Name _____

Address _____

City _____ State/Zip _____

VISA Card No. _____ Exp. Date _____

Signature _____ 155-07

FROM THE BESTSELLING AUTHOR OF THE

FINAL FRIENDS SERIES

Christopher Pike

No one does it better than Christopher Pike. His mystery and suspense novels are so fast-paced and gripping that they're guaranteed to keep you on the edge of your seat, guessing whodunit...

___ *LAST ACT* .... 73683/$3.50

___ *SPELLBOUND* .... 73681/$3.50

___ *GIMME A KISS* .... 73682/$3.50

___ *REMEMBER ME* .... 73685/$3.50

___ *SCAVANGER HUNT* .... 73686/$3.50

___ *FALL INTO DARKNESS* .... 73684/$3.50

From Archway Paperbacks

Simon & Schuster Mail Order Dept. CPS
200 Old Tappan Rd., Old Tappan, N.J. 07675

Please send me the books I have checked above. I am enclosing $_____ (please add 75¢ to cover postage and handling for each order. Please add appropriate sales tax). Send check or money order–no cash or C.O.D.'s please. Allow up to six weeks for delivery. For purchases over $10.00 you may use VISA: card number, expiration date and customer signature must be included.

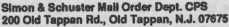

Name_____

Address_____

City_____ State/Zip_____

VISA Card No._____ Exp. Date_____

Signature_____ 159-08

Where Your Worst Nightmares Live...

R. L. Stine

— WELCOME TO FEAR STREET —

Don't listen to the stories they tell about Fear Street—stories about dark horrors and blood curdling cries in the night. Wouldn't you rather explore it yourself...and see if it's dark terrors and unexplained mysteries are true? You're not afraid, are you?

☐ *THE NEW GIRL* 70737/$2.95
☐ *THE SURPRISE PARTY* 73561/$2.95
☐ *THE OVERNIGHT* 73207/$2.95
☐ *MISSING* 69410/$2.95
☐ *THE WRONG NUMBER* 69411/$2.95
☐ *THE SLEEPWALKER* 69412/$2.95
☐ *HAUNTED* 70242/$2.95
☐ *HALLOWEEN PARTY* 70243/$2.95
☐ *THE STEPSISTER* 70244/$2.95
☐ *SKI WEEKEND* 72480/$2.95

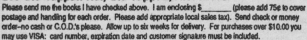

Simon & Schuster, Mail Order Dept. FSS
200 Old Tappan Rd., Old Tappan, N.J. 07675

Please send me the books I have checked above. I am enclosing $_____ (please add 75¢ to cover postage and handling for each order. Please add appropriate local sales tax). Send check or money order-no cash or C.O.D.'s please. Allow up to six weeks for delivery. For purchases over $10.00 you may use VISA: card number, expiration date and customer signature must be included.

Name_____

Address_____

City_____ State/Zip_____

VISA Card No._____ Exp. Date_____

Signature_____ 164-12